I0766352

Cry Silent

A Novel

Paperback ISBN: 978-1-63616-264-5
Hardcover ISBN: 978-1-63616-265-2
eBook ISBN: 978-1-63616-266-9

Published By Opportune Independent Publishing Co.
Cover Art by Sara Garza

Printed in the United States of America

For permission requests, please email the publisher with the subject line as "Attention: Permissions Coordinator" to the email address below:
Info@Opportunepublishing.com

DEDICATION

For the Survivors

Leola Jaines McGee was the picture of perfection amongst her peers. She was high school royalty, being the cousin of the city's wealthiest and most successful businessman—but she was carrying more than what meets the eyes. For as long as she could remember, Jaines had been dealt a bad hand in life, with her troublesome mother, her absentee father, and her elitist cousin Otis. She had learned to take her licks and keep on ticking. Jaines knew that being silent was the safest way to navigate the troubled waters of her world. But some secrets are just too heavy to carry, and some pains cut too deep to keep silent! After years of suppressing trauma, Jaines's hidden tears begin to bubble to the surface! Jaines did have a few allies, one being her overprotective big cousin Angela. Angela, once made aware of all the skeletons in Jaines's closet, goes on a rampage to protect her, and she's willing to take down anyone on her path to justice—even those she loves the most!

TABLE OF CONTENTS

ONE

"Shut up, and go sit down!" Mama said with frustration as she watched her favorite TV show. Tonight, it was the white man with the bimbo wife. She loved this show, something about a bigoted man who is married to a woman he loves-hates, with two children: an insignificant boy, and a bleach blond babe daughter who is dumb as a rock. I have no clue what the show is about. All I know is the characters and that when my mama is watching, I have to shut up and go sit down! *Note to self: Don't talk to Mama while she is watching her show. Other note to self: Just don't talk to Mama; it's better that way.*

Earlier today, we went to the Piggly Wiggly to get some fixings for dinner and some snacks for whenever. It was me and Mama. I tried to talk to her then, but she was busy reading her list and trying not to forget her ingredients for the salmon croquette she was making later. I had to "shut up and sit still in that basket" at the Piggly Wiggly too! That was twice today I had to shut up.

Note to self: Definitely don't talk to mama.

Whenever we went to the grocery store, I got to help box the groceries. The Piggly Wiggly doesn't use plastic; they use the leftover bottom box from canned good transports and big brown paper sacks. I loved going there because it meant I got to help box and bag the groceries. Mama was always particular about how it was done. This was one rare time when I could ask a question, and she would answer, because she liked her groceries a certain way. "Put all the canned goods together, and all the cold foods together. Keep all the common things close to one another. It's easier that way!"

"Like this, Mama?"

"Yes, baby, just like that," she would say. I would focus hard and try my best to place the groceries the right way so I could hear her say, "Good job, baby. See, you getting good at this now, ain't ya." *Note to self: Always help Mama at the* Piggly Wiggly, *and do it just right. Then, she'll say pretty things to me and make me feel seen.*

When we got home, my brother Jeston came out to help unload. He and Mama had a different type of thing going on; he could talk to Mama about whatever, whenever, and she always saw him, heard, him, and responded to him with pretty words. Not me though. The only people who talked pretty to me were my brother, my granny, and my third-grade teacher Mrs. Turner. Mrs. Turner would always say, "You sure look pretty today, Jaines," or "You're reading higher than all of your classmates, dear! That means you're smart!"

I liked school a lot. When the show was over, I was still shutting up and sitting down, while Mama moved to the kitchen to make her world-famous salmon croquette. It always tasted better than it smelled to me. Smelled like a river in hell, but it tasted like heaven, definitely her best meal. I was still scared to talk to her, so I just went to my side of the house and read my favorite book, *The Sisters Wild*.

We lived in a shotgun house on the corner, right across from the elementary school. Mama said it's called a shotgun house because you can stand at the front door and see straight through the back door, just like the barrel of a shotgun. I didn't like it; I didn't have my own room. My brother and I shared the middle section of the house. From the front door to the living room, you would have to walk straight through our space to get to the kitchen. It was a high-traffic area since anyone who came over had to walk through it just to get to the bathroom too. The bathroom was off to the right, and just before it was an open space, we used it as a closet. Our floors were rickety and made lots of noise and were weak in some places, and the foundation was so unleveled that you could see clear through the bathroom even when it was closed. Mama said to always put a towel in the crack when I took a bath so no one would see my private parts. There was only one other actual room in the house, which was Mama's room. It didn't have any doors, so she used sheets so we wouldn't be "all up in her business," as she would say. Mama said we lived in the ghetto and had to be careful of our surroundings because "anything could pop off at any minute." I liked the ghetto; it was fun at times and scary too.

"Jaines, put that book down and come fix your plate," Mama finally acknowledged me.

Because I was getting older, I had to start making my own plates, of course not without my mama hovering over my shoulder making sure I didn't get too much or that I wasn't "eating with my eyes." After I made my plate, I went back to my bed and ate my food. My brother was playing his video game and got to eat whenever he was good and ready. He was in the tenth grade, so I guess tenth-graders can do what they want.

Note to self: I can't wait to get to tenth grade.

"Leola Jaines McGee, you better not waste a damn thing in that bed, little girl."

"Yes, ma'am." I said with certainty! I knew not to say anything else, or it would be World War 3. I just left it at that. Leola Jaines McGee—that is my name. I hate it! Most people call me Jaines; they say "Leola" is too old of a name for someone as young and adorable as me. I like Jaines better anyway. Leola was my great great granny who I never met, and Jaines is my daddy's name. Never met him either. Mama says he is away on a long vacation; big brother says he is in prison for trying to murder Mama. I don't know which is the truth. All I know is I've seen pictures and we have the same eyes, same nose, same forehead—the exact same face. Except I got my mama's big lips. My brother said Daddy was mean and crazy and liked to stay out late at night doing the devil's work. Mama said Daddy was the kind of man that had a taste for trouble but tried his best to be good. Mama made me promise to forget about him and stop asking when he was coming home from vacation. But how can I forget about a man I look just like? And if she wanted me to forget him, why'd she give me his name? Somebody answer that! Couldn't ask Mama that though, uh-uh! That would be the end of me! I just keep silent, I just shut up and sit down, I just shut up and be still, I just shut up and obey.

It's better that way.

We woke up late the next morning for school, and all I could think was, *Hurry, Jaines! Don't make Mama mad, little girl.*

I hurried and brushed my teeth, put on my clothes, got on my shoes, and had my backpack on my back. I sat at the front door waiting for my big brother.

"Jaines, where you think you going with your head looking like that, little girl?" my mama yelled from her room. "Get in here so I can fix your hair, and hurry up!"

I ran to her room because I was "hurrying up" and accidentally knocked over her table with her ivory plants on it. I crashed into it so hard and fast that I went down, and the table did too. Her plants went flying and water splashed everywhere!

"Dammit, little girl! I swear your little ass is always messing up something. Now pick up my damn table."

I tried to hurry and pick up her table and put it back together the best I could. But my best wasn't good enough. Not this morning, not when Mama was late to work and Jeston might be late to school, since his bus was on the way. Mama didn't have time to fuss over her table, thank God; she just snatched my hair up into a quick ponytail and brushed my head with all of her frustration. But I knew not to say a word.

"Just shut up and take it, Jaines," I told myself.

Just then, Jeston yelled, "Jainey, let's go, girl! Don't make me miss the bus."

We lived right across from the elementary school. Jeston had to walk me to school before he got on his bus, which was convenient because the high school bus stopped just a block down from my school.

As we were walking out the door, Jeston said, "Here, take off that wet shirt and put this one on." While I was changing, he could see the panic on my face and said, "My little Jainey, take a deep breath. Everything's okay. Mama don't mean nothing that she do; she just can't help it."

I took my deep breath like my brother said, and I put on my dry shirt, and we headed out the door. At school, my hair was too tight; by the time I got to reading class with Mrs. Turner, I had a headache, and I asked Mrs. Turner if I could take a nap in the reading corner.

"Now, Jaines, why would I let you sleep during reading class, when everyone else has to read?" said Mrs. Turner.

"I have a headache. Honest. I really do." My teacher knew me not to tell tall tales.

"Okay. Go lay in the corner for a few minutes, then you have to get to reading these books."
I had no idea she would call Mama and tell her I had a headache in class that kept me from doing my work. I found out when I got home though. If I had known for even one second that Mrs. Turner was a traitor, I never would have liked her so much.

As soon as I walked in the door from school, I could hear Mama in the kitchen fixing something. Smelled like fried chicken; my tummy started growling at the smell of it.

Jeston walked in right behind me and said, "Mama, you cooking chicken?" Mama didn't respond to him, I think for the first time in forever.

"Jaines, bring your ass in here, girl."

Oh, man. I'm in trouble. My palms immediately began to sweat, and my mouth dried up. It's like all my spit just turned right into cotton. That walk to the kitchen was the longest walk ever. I tried to take slow steps as I mentally prepared myself for what was to come. *Whatever it is, just shut up and take it, Jaines. You can cry, but make sure you cry silent*, I reminded myself.

One time, Mama jacked me up by my ponytail for spilling my water on her "brand-new wood floors" that were really recycled laminate from Cousin Otis and were already scratched up and dented. When she snatched me up, it scared me, so I screamed and started to cry. Then, she said, "Oh, you think that's something? I'll give you something to cry for!"

Then, she whooped me with the belt until she got tired. I had to stay home from school for four days, and I couldn't sit on my bottom for almost a week. From that moment on, I learned to cry silent by keeping my tears and my screams on the inside and never letting them out.

Two more steps and I would be in the kitchen. I was so scared—honest, I was. As soon as I walked into the kitchen, I felt the sting of her hand impacting the right side of my face. She smacked me so hard, I temporarily forgot where I was.

"There, now you got a reason to have a headache. And don't you ever have your teacher call me about no shit like that again. You hear me?"

But I couldn't really hear her through the sound of my ears ringing, the burn of my face stinging, and the pain of my heart breaking. Jeston ran in the kitchen yelling, "Mama, her head hurt because you did her hair too tight! Now you gon' slap her for no reason?"

Jeston to the rescue!!!

My big superhero brother scooped me up into his arms and ran out the door down the street to Granny's house. My granny lived two blocks away around the corner on Lackland Street, in the shabby little house smack in the center of the cul-de-sac. My brother was so mad that he ran all the way there crying and gripping me as tight as he could. I kept looking behind him to see if Mama was coming. With my face still stinging and my ears still ringing, it felt like my nose was bleeding, but it may have just been fear running out of my skin. I was scared what would happen if Mama caught us. She was gon' beat me some more, and maybe even Jeston too. But she never came! Granny opened the door to the terror on Jeston's face.

"Boy, why you in a panic?"

"Mama just slapped little Jainey for no reason. She always hitting on her for nothing, Grandma. I can't let her do it no more." He handed me to my granny and ran off.

I didn't see him for a week after. My granny took me in and wiped my face and put a bag of frozen peas on my cheek.

"It's okay, my sweet baby girl. Granny gon' make it all better."

Turns out the fear running down my face was blood after all. Once she cleaned me up, she made me hot chocolate with marshmallows and sat me on her lap, squeezing me tight, humming a sweet tune in my ear, rocking me until I forgot about my stinging face and broken heart. She hummed, squeezed, and rocked the fear right out of my soul.

When I woke up, it was the next morning, and I was still at Granny's house. I jumped out of bed and ran to the kitchen to Granny, asking if I was late for school. Granny said I had to stay home today until the bruise on my face healed up. She said the teachers wouldn't understand how such a big, nasty bruise got on my tiny, cute face. Granny always called me cute; she said I was her little chocolate princess. I liked it when she said that. Granny told me not to worry and pulled some books out of her closet for me. She told me to go read at the table while she made breakfast. Later that day around noon, my mama came banging on Granny's door, asking where I was.

"Laney, she ain't coming back to you until you get your shit together. You ain't about to be whoopin' on my damn grandbaby like you ain't got no sense. Now, get the hell off my porch before I call the police and tell 'em whatcha did to her. Damn girl can't even go to school because you messed up her face. Get the hell off my porch, Laney. I raised you better!"

"Give me my goddamned baby, Mama. You can't take her from me. That's my baby, dammit! A little whooping never hurt nobody!" Mama yelled.

Granny rushed into the kitchen, grabbed the cordless phone off the wall, and threatened to call the police if she didn't leave. "She got the bruise on her face to prove it. Don't make me do this, Laney."

Mama left! But before she left, she yelled out, "Jaines, I love you, baby girl! Don't let nobody tell you nothing different!" She'd never told me she loved me before. I wasn't sure how to take it. *Note to self: Mama loved me, except she only realized it when someone took me from her!*

I didn't see Mama for almost a month. A week later, Jeston stopped by and brought me some gummy bears and some of my favorite things from Mama's house.

"How you doing, little Jainey?"

He always called me Jainey; it's like he couldn't remember my name ended in a S and not a Y. But I liked it when he called me Jainey.

"I brought you some stuff, and Mama is trying to get it together so you can come back home. She promised me she wasn't gon' hit you no more."

Jeston hugged me tight and kissed my cheeks and promised to come back to play goldfish with me tomorrow. I think promises are the things people say but don't mean. Like when my mama said she promised she wouldn't be mean to her baby girl no more, but she kept on; like when my cousin Otis promised he wouldn't touch me in my private places no more, but he kept on. Or like when I promised Mama I wouldn't think about my daddy no more, but I kept right on. I am learning that a promise is the same as a lie!

My brother lied. He didn't come back; in fact, I didn't see him again for years. For the next couple of months, I stayed with my granny, and she loved me good and took great care of me. Every time I asked a question, Granny answered with pretty words and in a pretty tone. She always made me cookies on Fridays and let me watch movies after 8 p.m. on the weekends. She gently brushed my hair and always told me how pretty I was. Granny was like a hero; she made my world safe. I missed my mama though.

I didn't miss her beatings, but I missed those rare moments of affirmation at the Piggly Wiggly, and the times when she did see me. Often my mother would stop by, and Granny would let us sit on the porch, and she would do my hair and make me promises or tell me lies, whichever it was.

"I promise I am gon' get myself together and get you back, little girl. I promise I love you; I promise I didn't mean to ever hurt you. I promise you are my sweet little Jaines."

Mama lied. She never got herself together. In fact, my granny told me she was a such a mess that she had to go on a long vacation for a while until she got better. I was hoping that she and Daddy were on the same vacation and that maybe they would find each other and come back together. *Note to self: Never hope; hoping is meaningless.*

———

One Sunday morning, I woke up and started getting ready for church, and noticed I didn't smell Granny's bacon or hear any gospel music blasting from the great room.

I called out, "Granny! Granny! You gon' cook us some breakfast?"

Granny didn't answer. I went looking for her and couldn't find her nowhere. I searched all over the house, and I couldn't find her. I couldn't call Mama since she was on vacation; my brother had gone missing; Cousin Otis lived not too far, but I was scared of his hands touching my private parts. I was scared and didn't know who to call. Jeston once told me that if I am ever scared or badly hurt, if I can get to a phone, call 911, and they will help me. I did. When they arrived, they took me outside and put me in the police car and told me not to worry; everything was going to be okay. I sat as they searched. After a while, I saw them rolling in the big bed on wheels! I had watched enough TV to know that's the bed they put hurt people on when they need to go to the hospital.

I could hear some mumbling on the dispatcher as they wheeled the bed back out with a white sheet covering somebody up. Right when I saw the sheet, I knew it was my granny, and I knew it wasn't good because she wasn't moving or talking or saying, "Everything is going to be okay, baby."

"Is that my Granny? Is she okay?"

I broke loose from the police car and bolted towards my granny, reaching for that white sheet, screaming "Granny, Granny, wake up!!"

Just as I was about to pull that white sheet off of her, the wind whisked me off my feet into the air! Only it wasn't the wind; it was a fireman. He cradled me into his arms and forced my face into his chest so I couldn't see. He didn't say nothing, just rocked me and patted my back like my granny used to do when she was trying to calm me down. But I couldn't calm down. I needed answers, so I kicked and screamed and fought with him, but he was too strong. He placed me in the back of the police car and buckled me in as I was kicking and screaming and crying. He never said a word, never got mad, just let me kick him and punch him and scream right in his face. Before he left, he looked at me and said, "Sometimes, God allows things we don't understand, but we have to trust Him anyway. Little lady, this is a time when you will have to just trust God. I am so sorry, sweetie."

And with a kiss on my forehead, he left me.

Before the police car drove away, a lady police joined me in the back seat. She was nice enough to let me cry on her shoulders. She said pretty words to me like, "Baby girl, everything will be fine. We will make sure you get to a safe place." But I didn't care what she said. Something was wrong with my granny, and they wouldn't tell me, just kept lying to me.

"Is my granny dead? How come she wasn't moving? Was that my granny on that bed?"

"Sweetheart, don't worry about anything. We are going to take you to your nearest relative, and they will explain everything."

What she didn't know is that I didn't have any nearest relatives; it was only my mama, my brother, and my granny—and cousin Otis, who lived not too far away. But I'd never met another relative. I was hoping Mama was back and I could go with her, or Jeston had turned up and I could go with him. *Anybody but Cousin Otis. Please, not Otis.*

Then, I remembered not to hope, because it was meaningless. As the day turned into night, the police dropped me off at a place that looked like the places you see in sad movies where kids with no parents get left at. Some tall white lady with smeared red lipstick on her teeth came and knelt down right in front of me and tried to look me in my eyes, but I slammed them shut as tight as I could!

"Good evening, Ms. McGee. I hear you're having a tough day. Well, I hope I can make it better for you; my name is Tan Hall, and I'll be handling your case. How are you feeling right now?"

I didn't answer.

"I see that you're in the third grade, headed to fourth. Am I correct?"

I didn't answer, just squeezed my eyes shut tighter.

"Sweetie, I understand you are upset. Is there anything I can do to make you feel better?"

I didn't respond, just shut my eyes tighter and folded my arms and stomped my foot on the floor, hoping that would make her run away!

"The sooner we can get some information from you, the sooner we can inform you about your grandmother."
She said the magic words!

"Yes," I mumbled under my breath.

"Okay. Thank you, Leola—"

"Jaines. Everybody calls me Jaines," I sternly interrupted.

"Okay. So, it's like James, but with an N?"

I nodded my head yes.

"Okay, sweetie. I have some news to share with you. Your grandmother was injured in your home today as she was entering her basement. Unfortunately, the doctors were unable to help her. She has passed away."

There is this place I like to go to in my mind when I am so hurt I can't stand it, or when I can't think. I used to go to that place a lot with Mama when she used to haul off and smack me or jack me by my ponytails. I like to go to that place when Otis makes me pull down my panties and touch my privates with his privates. I go to that place when things don't make sense. Nothing exists in that place. It's a silent place—no noise, no color, no movement, no feelings, no tears. I'm only in third grade, but my mama taught me how to get to a lot of places in my mind, and Otis too. Some light places and some dark places. Some safe places and some unsafe places. This place is the safest one though; I usually stay here until I realize everything outside of me is okay and I can exist again.

I like this place. I think I'll stay here for now.

"Leola. Leola, baby, can you hear me? She's not responding; she's in shock." I could hear Mrs. Hall talking, but I couldn't respond. I was in my place, and I wasn't coming out.

People were moving all around me and talking and flashing lights in my eyes, snapping their fingers in my face, yelling my name. I could see them and hear them, but I couldn't come out of my place to talk to them. I could hear a voice in me say, "Jaines, talk." But I ain't talking, I ain't thinking, I ain't feeling. Without my granny, it's not safe enough to exist!

After hours of seeing and hearing people do what they were doing, they decided I needed real help. I was led off to a room that was white, with a bed that had white sheets. There were a few machines that made beeping noises. After I was settled onto the thin bed and tucked in by some lady nurse, they let me rest. I slept for hours, not waking up until the next day.

"Leola, sweetheart, can you hear me?"

The lady nurse was standing over me, gazing down with a genuine smile. Mrs. Hall was standing right behind her, looking at me curiously like she was wondering if I was going to talk today. I wasn't!

Mrs. Hall knelt down beside my bed and looked me in

the eyes. "Baby girl, we have found your nearest relative, and we will send you with him as soon as we get you all better. Your grandmother's service will be in a few days; you can go see her one last time if you improve."

Did she say I could see my granny one last time? Wait, will she be talking? Will I get to hug her neck and smell her scent? Will she tell me I am her little chocolate princess? But didn't she die? Don't they put dead people in the dirt? Can dead people talk?

I had so many questions, but I couldn't ask because I was in my place, and I wasn't ready to leave.

"Baby, can you hear me?"

I didn't respond.

"She isn't getting any better. We will have to tell her cousin Otis that she has to stay with us for a while until she is able to process this trauma." Mrs. Hall was telling the nurse I would be there until I could talk and get better. I heard her say "Otis," but I couldn't make out the rest. I think I might have to come out of my place soon. I have too many questions.

TWO

One day, Mama got called into work, and my brother had a sports thing, and Granny was at bingo, so I needed a sitter. We lived in the ghetto, so it wasn't safe to just "stay with no any-damn-body," my mama would say. She said it's better to stay with close friends and relatives. But we didn't have any. Ever since we moved here to North Carolina from Chicago, we didn't have really close people. But my cousin Otis did live about fifteen miles down the road, and Mama said, "Now Cousin Otis, that's a cousin I can trust."

She took me there on the days she had to work and I had no sitter. Otis lived in a gentrified neighborhood; I only knew that because I heard Mama say it. "He has enough money to live in the Hills with the snooty white folks, but he chooses to live in the uppity hood with the Black folk," she would say.

His house was huge and surrounded by big windows. Mama said he had acreage, but I never knew what that meant. She said he was the only one in the family with land, so that made him the most valuable. Which explained why everyone treated him like a king. Whatever he asked for, he got it, and whatever he said do, people did. He was a tall, handsome man, with caramel brown skin and wavy hair. His eyes were light brown and had a wide almond shape; he had a deep voice that was sultry when he spoke. Every time he spoke, it was smooth and calming, like water flowing down a small stream. He always dressed in the finest suits. I never saw him in jeans. Never.

"Cousin O is the man around town" is what Jeston would always say. Jeston wanted to be just like him.

When I first started going to Otis's house, it was fun. He had a garden and a few chickens in his backyard that he let me feed. He also gave me a little spot in his garden for pink roses; he called it "Leola's Corner." I would beg Mama to let me go over on days I didn't need a sitter so I could water my roses and trim my weeds. Cousin Otis said weeds are bad and we had to keep them out. Otis didn't have any kids, but he was married to Angela, and she was pretty. Angela was tall, with silky chocolate skin; her head was full of wild, curly coils of hair that fell however they wanted. She called it "natural." I wished I had her hair.

Angela was so nice. We had tea parties in the garden and used to pick fresh veggies and make salads and fresh juice. But Angela was a lawyer who was always working and often out of town. Cousin Otis was a business owner. Seemed like everybody knew Cousin Otis, and they called him "Big O." I knew he was popular because he had a commercial and he always had company over talking business. When they talked business, I had to "go play," but he didn't have toys, so I just went to my roses and talked to them. He said flowers liked to talk and talking made them feel loved, and if they felt loved, then they would grow.

Cousin Otis's house was so much fun at first, until one day when Mama dropped me off. Otis told me to go play, even though he didn't have any company, which I didn't understand. But I went to my garden anyway. I was in my garden for hours, telling mythological tales to my roses and hoping I would see them grow.

"Leola, come here, baby girl. I want to show you something."

I came running to Otis with a huge smile because anytime he said he wanted to show me something, that meant he had a present, a treat, or a prize for me for being so good. I was excited to see what he had for me today, probably because I was obeying and playing so good in the garden. But when I got to him, his hands were empty, and there was nothing around him that looked like a present. In fact, he was standing in the doorway of the hall restroom with his shirt off, and his belt was unbuckled. I was immediately scared because I'd never seen a man's chest before, and I never saw Cousin Otis without a business suit on. It felt wrong. I felt like I should run in the other direction, but I didn't. I stopped right in front of him. He stood in front of me, looking down at me, and he felt like a tower hovering over me.

For the first time ever, I was scared to look at him, which was strange because he'd never scared me before.

"Baby girl, look. I want to show you something."

I kept my head down.

"It's okay, little cousin. You know I would never hurt you, don't you?"

I was quiet, still uneasy.

He knelt down and grabbed my chin and gently lifted my

head up so I could look in his eyes. When we made eye contact, he smiled at me and caressed my face softly. I felt at ease, then remembered he was someone I could trust.

"I know you're scared, but just trust me. I won't hurt you, baby girl. I want to show you how much I love you."

I stood there silent, frozen, stuck.

"Look."

He pointed down to the middle of his pants, and they were bulging. Something was sticking straight out from the middle.

"What is that?" I asked out of sheer curiosity. The sound of my own voice shook me out of my fear.

"Here. Let me show you."

He unzipped his pants, pulled them down, and showed me his private place. I knew it was his private place because I accidentally walked in on Jeston peeing one time, and he had the same kind of private place. I knew it was his private place because Mama always told me to put the towel in the crack in the restroom door so nobody could see my privates, or my middle parts.

"My brother has one of those," I spoke.

"Yeah, I do too. Have you ever touched one?"

"No."

Cousin Otis grabbed my little eight-year-old hands and placed them on his middle part. I was nervous, so I jerked my hand back.

"It's okay, baby girl."

He grabbed my hand again and placed it back on his middle part. This time, he moved my hand back and forth. I was scared, so I closed my eyes.

"I'm scared," I said softly.

"Everybody is scared the first time they touch one, but remember, I am not going to hurt you. Has Cousin Otis ever hurt you?"

"No."

He was still moving my hand. My hand was so small compared to his anatomy. I wondered how this was love. I wondered why I needed this kind of love.

"Otis, where are you, baby? I'm home!"

Angela was home! Angela, my hero!

Immediately, Cousin Otis pulled up his pants and knelt down in front of me. He looked me square in the eyes and said, "Leola, my sweet baby girl, I love you. And this is our little secret, okay? Promise me you won't tell anyone about this. You promise?"

"Yes, sir."

"Now go on back to your garden and play, and I'll make you some lunch."

Then, he bolted out of the restroom, and I could hear him and Angela embracing and kissing in the hallway.

"Come on, baby. I missed you. Let me show you how much I missed you, girl."

I stood in the doorway of the restroom and watched Cousin Otis nibbling on Angela's ear as he pulled her up the stairs to the bedroom.

"Hey, Jaines, baby!" Angela yelled from the top of the stairs.

I couldn't respond!

For the first time in my life, I was afraid of a man. I was

scared and confused because Mama was usually the one who scared me. Cousin Otis never hurt me; he said he loved me. It must have been okay, right? Even though it felt wrong. He said it's our little secret. I was good at keeping secrets, because I never told anyone how Mama used to beat me, and how much I thought about my daddy. Guess I could keep this secret too, right? Mama had already taught me how to shut up. I decided I would just shut up and keep this secret because it was me and Cousin Otis's special thing. Besides, he was always so nice to me. Even though this felt wrong, it had to be right because Cousin Otis would never hurt me, right?

I was so wrong. That day was the beginning of my introduction to womanhood and the end of my childhood innocence. I just didn't know it.

———————

"Leola, we have found your nearest relative, and he is all ready to take you home. He says you are very close, and you'll do well there."

By this time, Mrs. Hall and the lady nurse were speaking to me in a room with a big round table, and some other people I didn't know. They all went around the table and introduced themselves, but I wasn't listening. I was too busy hoping this relative wasn't Cousin Otis.

"Jaines, we are going to bring your relative in and discuss the circumstances of your situation to make sure this is the best home for you to be placed in; is that okay with you?"

I didn't respond. I was deep in my place.

"Okay. Well, let's bring him in, and we can all get started then."

Mrs. Hall looked at me with so much hope. She paused and waited for me to respond. She was so hopeful; I guess she didn't know that hope was meaningless!

"Bring him in."

"Jaines, baby girl, how are you?"

It was OTIS!!!!!

The moment I saw his face, I tried to go deeper into my place, but I was already the deepest I could get in my mind. I tried to get there in the physical sense; my body melted out of my chair as I slithered to the floor in one swift move and hurried under the table, balling myself into the fetal position and tucking my head between my legs, hoping I could disappear. I tried so hard to disappear. I heard that voice inside me say, *Jaines, talk. You have to talk.* But I wouldn't!

"Jaines, baby girl, come from under that table. What's the matter?" I heard Angela's sweet, soft voice and remembered I was safe with her once, but could I trust her now?

"Baby, come here. I know you're hurting, sweetie. We all are, and it's okay. Come here, my princess."

Angela was so persistent, and her voice was so sweet. I needed her safety, and she was familiar. I slowly crawled from under the table and reached for her. She scooped me into her arms and kissed my cheeks; she rocked me and hummed a sweet melody in my ear. I cried on her breast as I inhaled her fancy perfume. It felt so good. *I could stay here; this may bring me out of my place.*

"Jaines, baby, how are you doing?"

It was Otis.

I didn't respond.

All the adults talked about my life and my condition for the next hour like I was not in the room. Angela was still holding me and rocking me; she rocked me to sleep.

"Leola is still in shock, and our psychologists believe she has suffered from other trauma. This place of shock is alarming and may be due to a culmination of unprocessed traumas. Leola needs intensive therapy; she needs a nurturing and calm environment and stability, which our caseworkers have determined you and your wife to be, Mr. McGee."

It had been decided I was going to Cousin Otis's house; I was asleep and so deep in my place that I could not speak and tell them that his house was the most unstable. But was too late. I was in trouble.

Pink-and-purple everything was everywhere. I guess Otis and Angela thought these were every little girl's favorite colors. They had a room ready for me when I arrived at their home; Angela boasted about decorating it, but it looked like cotton candy vomit. Perhaps I was just in a bad mood because I was back in this house that had so many secrets.

"This is your space, baby girl. You can draw, color, play dress-up, and do whatever makes you happy in here." Angela was giving me the rundown on my new paradise as she put away my things. She scooped me into her lap and laid my head on her chest and rocked me and hummed. "You know your granny is looking down on you from heaven, right?"

I didn't respond.

"She had a nice service, Jaines, and we have some things of hers to give you from her place. We took lots of pictures that you can look at whenever you are ready."

I didn't respond.

"Are you okay, baby? You can talk to me. You know that, right?"

Something about Angela made me feel so safe. I could sense the genuine love she had for me; it wasn't the kind of love like Otis gives or Mama gives. It was a love that reminded me of Jeston and Granny. I knew I was safe with her, so I came out of my place just for a second.

"I'm scared. What happened to Granny? I miss her! Where is my mama? What happened to my brother? I don't want to be here." Every question I had on my mind at the moment just came out. My own voice shocked me, and I remembered I wasn't ready to come out of my place. In haste, I retreated, vowing not to talk anymore that day. *Dammit! Now I have to feel; now I have to process all of the answers! Dammit, I am not ready!!*

Angela proceeded to answer every question in the order I asked. My granny accidentally fell down the steps when she was trying to take the laundry to the basement, and due to her being in her 80s, the fall was hard on her, and she suffered bleeding internally and didn't get help in time. She was dead all morning, and I didn't even know she was there. My mama was in a place called "prison," for stealing a man's credit card or something like that. Angela said she would be home in a few months, but it would be best for me not to return to her on account of how she used to treat me. Jeston ran away a few weeks after he ran me to Granny's house. I guess he was good at running. He was located by the police a few days later at his teacher's house. She took him in but called the authorities because she thought he was in danger. The authorities took him to a place called "juvie" so he could get back on track. Angela said he was only there for a few days, but when he was released, he went to live with his dad back in Chicago.

I was confused. I thought Daddy was on vacation, but I couldn't ask. I had already vowed not to talk anymore.

"Why don't you want to be here, princess? I thought you liked it here."

I was done talking.

"I promise Otis and I will do our best to get you back to yourself again. I am so sorry you have to go through all of this."

"I have to go on a business trip tomorrow for a few days, but when I return, we will have some girl time. We'll go shopping and get our nails painted. Does that sound like fun, sweetie?"

"Don't leave me here with Otis!" Please! He touches me inappropriately, and I don't like it. He makes me touch him, and I hate it. Please take me with you, Angela, please!!"

I wish I had the courage to say that to her. I said it with my eyes, and I hoped she would read them, but she didn't. Just kissed my forehead and tucked me into bed. *Note to self: Hope is still meaningless.*

"Baby, you know Jaines doesn't want to be here? Oh, yeah, she finally talked to me too."

"Really? What did she say?" Otis was standing, looking

out the window of his bedroom at his garden as he and Angela prepared for bed.

"She said she doesn't want to be here, then she looked at me with the saddest look I've ever seen. I wish I could read her mind; she stopped talking after she asked a few questions."

"Well, she has been through a lot, Angela. She has a lot going on in her little mind, and her heart is broken. Maybe being here reminds her of her granny or something, I don't know. She has no one now. We are all she has; she has nowhere else to go."

"What about her father in Chicago?"

"Laney made me promise I would never let her go to him if she was unable to care for her. Laney is like a sister to me; I can't let her down. It's bad enough that Jeston is with him. No telling how he's doing. I need to try to get him back too before Laney gets out."

"You really think we can raise two kids? Besides, he is almost grown anyway. And what's so bad about their father?"

"He tried to kill Laney when he found out she was pregnant with Leola. He wanted no parts of another baby. He set the house on fire with Jeston and Laney in it. Police could never prove it was him, but we know it was."

"So, he was never charged?" Angela inquired as she changed into her nightgown.

"Not for that, but he was arrested later on some other stuff. And yes, I think we can raise two kids. We are rich; money is all we need. Whatever we can't do, a nanny can."

"Babe, that's so horrible. You know that's how I was raised, and I hated it. These kids have been through enough. If we are going to take care of them, then they deserve our best. I can become a stay-at-home mom; that's always been a dream of mine, anyway."

Otis and Angela discussed my life well into the night until they fell asleep. He never told her our secret. He never once told her his special way of showing me love.

THREE

George Washington Carver Academy, the school of uppity Black folk and even more uppity white folk. Another place I don't fit into. All my life, I've been wanting to get to tenth grade, and now that I am here, it's hard to believe I still can't do what I want. When Jeston was in tenth grade, he did whatever he wanted. He even ran away, and nobody stopped him. If I tried to run away, it would be the end of the world. I would run away too if I knew where to run to. I can't think of a single solitary place that is safe for a girl like me to run to. "A girl like you." That's what Cousin Otis always says when he is ranting and raving about why I can't go to this party or hang out at that place.

I'm not allowed to do anything but read books and water my roses. "A girl like you isn't safe in this world; a girl like you is too pretty to be out alone late at night; a girl like you can't be trusted in a room full of young boys."

What, like I'm a whore or something. I wish I had the guts to stand up to Otis, but I just shut up and take it! Now that I am in the tenth grade, my body is changing rapidly, and I don't even understand the attention I get around here. Every boy just gawks at me, and all the girls hate me. Except for Elizaveth; she is my Dominican sister from another mister. We have the same body type, so we go through the same shit. They say we are sluts, "girls that look like they love boys," which couldn't be further from the truth. We are actually both virgins who are deathly afraid of the thought of some boy's nasty penis. YUCK!! I gag at the thought. From the time my granny died until now, I have "blossomed like a beautiful flower," according to Angela. My legs are long and thick, my hips are nice and shapely, not too wide, my waist is small, and I have a "nice, round booty," according to Elizaveth.

Not to mention, my breasts are full and perky; I skip out on bras many days because I don't like the sensation of the wire. Even without a bra, they stand right up. Elizaveth always jokes that I am the epitome of the "Coke bottle shape" that men love and women envy. Since my hair is natural like Angela's and mostly wound in tight, coily curls, it's hard to manage. I typically wear a sleek bun and lay my baby hairs down nicely. But the cheer team is taking photos today, and Angela said I should get a Dominican blowout and "really show those hating bitches who's boss."

She's so funny. I always vent to her about how the girls at school hate me; she says it's because I am beautiful and they wish they had my chocolate brown skin and angel eyes. I've never noticed my beauty; I've been too busy hiding it and trying to be invisible. When I was in ninth grade, Angela noticed I was awkwardly shy and encouraged me to join the cheer squad. I dreaded the thought of parading myself around in front of thousands of people, or even going to football games. The skirts were too short, the tops were too tight, and I just hate being looked at. I hate it. "You are a stunner, just like your mama used to be," is what Otis says. "A girl like you is supposed to be desired."

I hate him! But I am glad I joined the team. Without the team, I would not have met Elizaveth, and I would never have a reason to leave my room or escape my hell.

Last week, Angela took me to the hair shop in Little Havana to get my blowout. All the thugs in Little Havana love to see me and Angela coming. They whistle and holler and flash their dope money, trying to impress us like they didn't just see us get out of a three-hundred-thousand-dollar McLaren. Angela always told me, "Don't be impressed by bad guys and their money. You need a good guy like your Cousin O."

Ha! She is sweet but also dumb as a rock if she thinks her husband is good. One of these days, I'll work up the courage to tell her that he has regular afternoon love sessions with me when she is away on business. Just last week, he locked me in my room for two days after he invaded my privacy and read my diary, which detailed all the ways I hate how he shows love and how I planned to tell my school counselor about how he sneaks into my room at night and puts his hands in my panties. I no longer have a diary; he said he burned it. I no longer have access to the internet; he said it's too dangerous for a girl like me who has the pressure of keeping so many secrets. If only I could stand up to him. I thought that as I got older, I would get stronger, but being locked in my room for two days with no phone and being denied food and restroom privileges made me realize I am at his mercy.

After having to use an empty Pringles can as a toilet and eating old, crusty gummy bears I found behind my bed, I thought about jumping out of the window. But it's a huge two-story mansion with a concrete patio below my room. I'm sure this setup was a maniacal strategy. Otis was diabolical. I learned that he is a top business analyst in the city; everyone who is anyone comes to him for help with their businesses. He has three local firms and one in Asia that he uses to outsource work. He was on the *Forbes* Top 40 Under 40 list, and recently won Businessman of the Year.. He really is "the man around town." I have a plan to expose him, and soon, I will have the courage to execute it.

———————————

Shoot! I am gonna be late.

"Wait! Don't close the door."

I was sprinting down the hallway to my algebra class. Just as I was about to reach the door, I smacked right into another student, knocking him off his feet. His papers and books went flying everywhere. Like a ricochet, I went flying off my feet in the opposite direction.

"Jaines McGee, you're late again, missy. I'm sure your cousin Otis would not be too pleased about this." My teacher, Mr. Rangel, was smirking at me from the doorway.

"Please, please, don't tell him. I am sorry. I was on time, but this guy, he just came out of nowhere and knocked me down, sir."

"Actually, you knocked him down, Speedy. There is no running in the hallway!"

Mr. Rangel was the rudest old man you'd ever meet. He didn't even bother to help us up, just stood there making his point. He was an obnoxious old know-it-all who never lost an argument. He and Otis were business buddies who were a part of the same country club; they played golf and gossiped about me every Sunday. He thinks he is a part of my family, which I take full advantage of. I hate his class, so I am always late on purpose. He never follows through with his empty threats to tell on me.

Me and the other kid slowly gathered our things and got to our feet. I was busy dusting my uniform off when I heard the sweet sound of my name.

"Jaines."

I looked up and locked eyes with the most beautiful boy I've ever seen.

"Who are you? I'm sorry, I mean, what's your name? My name is Jaines. I'm so sorry for bumping into you. I mean, hi, nice to meet you."

I was nervous and making a fool of myself.

"Hi, Jaines. I'm Andre, and it's nice to meet you too."

"Um … Um, don't you have somewhere to be?" Mr. Rangle said, rudely interrupting my stargaze. Andre and I quickly made it to our seats without taking our eyes off each other. Who was he? How did he know my name? I wondered as I focused on how beautifully his caramel skin paired with his hazel eyes and thick, wavy low-cut fade.

"Damn, he's so fine," I whispered to myself before letting fantasies of our wedding day carry me through the rest of the class hour.

I had pictures directly after school today. When algebra was over, I raced to the locker room to prep and prim; I flat-ironed any fuzzies out of my hair and put on my makeup. The pictures took about an hour. When we were finished, Cousin Otis was waiting outside to pick me up. He was on the phone as I approached the car, so he couldn't immediately see how I looked. Otis was out of town for a week and didn't know Angela had my hair pressed. I've been growing my hair since childhood, unrelaxed and with no chemicals. When it was straight, it fell to the middle of my back, just above my waistline. Today Elizaveth said, "Listen chica, all Black women are beautiful, but none are as beautiful as you, mami."

I wished I could agree with her. When I got in the car, Otis was still on the phone and did not look at me. As we headed down the street, he ended his call and finally looked in my direction. Just then, I remembered I had on makeup. I usually remember to take it off before I get home from games.

Dammit. I messed up.

"Jaines, baby girl, who gave you permission to straighten your hair?" Otis questioned me without looking in my direction.

"Angela."

"Who gave you permission to wear makeup?"

"Um, nobody did, sir; I just have to since I am in cheer. We took pictures today."

Otis instilled a special type of fear in me. It was a confusing fear. On one hand, I knew he loved me because he took me in and provided a very comfortable life for me. He took me out of the ghetto into a gated community in the Hills; he pays for my private school and already has a G Wagon waiting for my sixteenth birthday. Sometimes he tells me sweet things and encourages me when I am afraid. Sometimes he cooks me the best meals, and he even let me expand "Leola's corner" to add more vegetables and fruits. He takes me on shopping sprees, and I've been to more countries than anyone in my grade level. Otis is kind, loving, and tender. He even lets me see my mother and has taken me to hang with my brother. But he hurts me too; he controls every aspect of my life. He wants to control my every thought. He lies to me and forces me to lie to myself. He makes me do things to him that I now know are wrong because the school counselors told us they are during the abuse seminar we had last week. This is fear with mixed emotions. I'm scared of how much power he has over me. *Note to self: Love hurts, and men with power are dangerous.*

I was afraid to look at him as we talked. I know he was giving me a mad stink eye because I could feel a hole burning into the side of my face.

"So, your coach told you that you had to wear make-up?"

"Mm-hmm." I nodded my head yes.

I was lying; fear made me lie. I was still not looking at him. "Didn't you just hear me say nobody told me to wear it, dummy?" I wish I had the courage to say that.

He handed me his phone

"Call your coach."

"Why?" I said out of shock.

"Don't question me, Leola. Just do it."

Oh, shit. He called me Leola. He only does that when he's mad.

I called my coach.

"Hello, this is Coach Marks."

"Yes, this is Otis McGee, Jaines's cousin."

"Yes, sir, I know who you are. How can I help you?"

"I'm just calling to let you know she will no longer be participating in cheer. She will return her belongings to you tomorrow."

Click.

He hung up!

Dammit. I shouldn't have lied.

I was just about to cry real tears when I remembered that whooping Mama gave me as a child, so I just kept them in and cried silently.

"I will deal with Angela about your hair when she gets home. As soon as we get to the house, you need to wash it out."

"Shut up! I will not wash it out. I will not go home with you. I hate you! I wish you were dead!" I almost said it out of sheer rage, but I knew better. I kept my mouth shut, and I obeyed.

"Yes, sir."

"That's my girl." Otis was smiling and rubbing my inner thigh. "I have something to show you when we get home."

Angela's business trip would be over in two days, and she would be home. I hated when she left on business. I wished she would go back to staying at home like she did when I was young. Angela worked part time from home for five years after she and Otis first took me in. When she was at home, I was safe, and Otis was the best big cousin ever; he didn't touch my privates at all. When I got to ninth grade, she said I was old enough to look after myself for short periods of time, so she went back to working full time. Angela was a big deal. She won all of her cases with the exception of one. The client was kidnapped during the trial, never to be seen again. Angela still cries about that sometimes.

When people are in trouble, they call Angela. And she has a heart for her people; she will help anyone, even if they can't pay. She specializes in cases where cops unjustly shoot people, especially the disenfranchised. She is good at her job too; I've gotten to see her in action several times. Sometimes when she had to go into trial, she would let me sit in the office. It had a camera in it that filmed all the action in the courtroom. Angela did not take anybody's mess; she was so passionate. I decided I wanted to be a lawyer just like her when I grow up. Angela was the only woman Otis really respected; he bowed down to her and did whatever she asked him to do. It was like she had him in a trance.

She said when I get older, she would tell me all about how she has my cousin so whipped. Whatever that means. I loved her, and she loved me. She was my hero. When she was away, Otis would take my phone so I couldn't call her, and then he'd lie to her and tell her I was busy all week doing projects and homework. I really wanted to warn her about the hair thing so she'd know it wasn't my fault. I also wanted to tell her he made me quit cheer. I needed to talk to her, or somebody. I was afraid of going back to that safe place in my mind. It took me two years to come out of my place after my granny died. I went to therapist after therapist and tried all of the medical trials Otis and Angela could pay for. Nothing was working until they took me to the "Spiritual Guru."

She's an old church lady in our neighborhood who has a reputation for spiritual healing. I spent a week at her house; Otis paid her five thousand dollars to "fix me." Angela stayed at the house with me to watch the Guru and make sure she "wasn't doing no freaky shit," as she would say. "I will do whatever it takes to get you back, princess," is what she promised me. *I need Angela right now. I need somebody.*

What I didn't need was Otis's special love. I thought about running away to Elizaveth's house, but if I did, Otis would just find me and make life worse.

I wasn't having Otis's hands on my body tonight; I just had to figure out a way to keep him off me. I couldn't run away. I couldn't call 911. I only had one option.

———————

When we got to the house, Otis told me to wash up and get ready for bed, and he would come and tuck me in. But I knew what that meant. "Tuck me in" was his special way of saying "put my hands in your panties."

"Yes, sir," I obeyed.

I went to my room and wrote two letters, one for Angela and one for Elizaveth. I hope they find them.

Tonight, I decided to take a bath. I haven't taken one in a long time. I prefer showers, but I think a bath is the best way to get clean before I die. When they find me, I want my body to be really clean. Our house was huge; it had ten rooms and six bathrooms. O said it's for guests, but we never had guests. My mama said it's for show, and boy, what a show "Big O" was; he was the fakest ever. Smiling and grinning in everyone's face when all along, he is sexually violating his little cousin on almost a daily basis! I hate him!

As I walked into my luxury bathroom with marble floors and granite countertops, I marveled at the beautiful crystal chandeliers hanging from the ceiling. They were my favorite luxury; I know I'll miss them. I searched my medicine cabinet for anything that would make me die. Tylenol, Advil, Excedrin, Midol, vitamins. No, I needed something stronger. I couldn't find anything. I kept rummaging through all my drawers, and finally, I asked O If I could get some Advil from his medicine cabinet.

He said yes.

I calmly and quietly searched his cabinets for anything that would make me die. Looked like he didn't have shit either, until I stumbled upon a bottle of Xanax and a bottle of oxycodone. Wonder why they had this. Doesn't matter; it's exactly what I needed. I went back to my room to make sure my letters were still where I left them.

They were.

Back in the bathroom, my tub was full and steaming. Before I died, I wanted to say a prayer to God.

I knelt beside the tub, then bowed my head and closed my eyes like my granny taught me.

"Dear God, I don't know why You chose me for this life. I have always heard heaven was the best place to go. Angela said my granny is there. I really miss her, and I really want to be free. I hope heaven is as nice as people say it is. Do mothers hit their daughters there? I hope not. Do cousins touch private places there? I hope not. I hope You will know who I am when I get there. I hope that hope is not meaningless in heaven. Oh, and can You tell my granny I am on my way? It would be nice if You could have her standing at the gates to walk me in, because I am really scared of walking in alone. Thank You for listening, God. I'll see You really soon. Amen."

I took every pill left in both bottles: six xanax, four oxycodone. I hopped in the tub and scrubbed my body as hard as I could in every place, especially my privates. I tried to wash away every time Otis touched me there!

My skin started to burn as I rinsed myself off.

Maybe I scrubbed too hard.

After a while, I started to feel loose, like my muscles were melting. I tried to speak, but I couldn't. I tried to find the clock so I could see my time of death, but my eyes were hard to move. I was numb. I could feel my thoughts slowing down and every feeling fading away, and I was relieved that Otis wouldn't get me this time.

I rested the back of my head on the tub as I slipped into nothingness.

Fuck you, Otis. I win!

FOUR

"Hello? Hey, babe—"

"Angela, Jaines is hurt. You need to get home now."

Click.

"Wait, what? What's going on? Hello? Otis? Hello?"

Dammit!

Jaines was the apple of Angela's eye. She had reminded her of someone she lost a long time ago. Ever since she was a little girl, she has adored her big, brown almond eyes and her silky chocolate skin. Jaines had the biggest smile with the most perfect teeth. Angela was always surprised she came out so beautiful, given that her mother was on crack the whole time she was pregnant with her.

What the hell is wrong with my baby girl? I gotta get home right now, she thought to herself.

Angela was away on business, helping fight a high-profile case in New Orleans. A cop thought a young sixteen-year-old Hispanic male had a weapon in his pocket that turned out to be a cell phone. The cop has already been charged with his murder. Now, Angela is with the boy's family and the district attorneys, seeking the harshest punishment allowed for his crime in that state. Angela was going for life; the parents wanted death.

Angela believed in grace and was not an eye-for-an-eye type of woman. Forgiveness was ingrained in her from a young age by her mother and her father. "Forgiveness is the only way to have peace," her daddy would say. She makes it a practice to forgive wrongdoers immediately, except for crimes against children, which is why she still hasn't forgiven her parents. She had a soft spot for the weak and vulnerable and hated anyone who violated a child. However, in this case, she still couldn't muster up enough hatred to seek death and felt the officer may have genuinely been afraid for his life. They were just hours away from the judge's decision, and she didn't want to leave. She needed to hear for herself. But Otis was urging her to come home.

Angela tried calling Otis back several times, but he would not answer.

Angela, baby, it's not good. Get here fast, he texted.

Otis's text scared Angela. She knew she had to go.

Angela was the daughter of Leeland and Deborah Chambers. Leeland was the sole heir of his father's millions. Leeland's father was an inventor who made millions selling his inventions to major corporations. He was an only child due to the death of his older sister in a skydiving freak accident. Upon her death, his father changed his will, leaving Leeland the sole heir of his fortune. Leeland was a wise man who was taught the value of a dollar. When he inherited his father's fortune, he immediately began to invest and made very profitable returns. Leeland, through his investments, was able to triple his father's millions. However, he became obsessed with making more and more money. He was either traveling with investors or researching new ways to expand his profits. Either way, he had no time for Angela. Angela's mother was a selfish snob of a woman, always finding new ways to spend her father's millions.

Angela's parents were too consumed with their own lives to really focus on how she was growing up. She had a live-in nanny who was her primary caregiver. Her nanny was distant and standoffish, clearly just collecting a check. However, she did manage to make sure Angela was overly involved in extracurricular activities, primarily because she wanted no parts of her. Angela was regularly rotating between gymnastics, dance, cheer, and the "Young Equestrians Club." If she wasn't perfecting her double roundhouse, she was learning to tame the emotions of Ninnie the horse. Angela lived a life in the lap of luxury; everything she wanted, she got it. But what she yearned for the most, money couldn't pay for, and she never recieved.

All Angela ever needed and wanted was love, affection, and quality time with her parents. But between her mother's extravagant trips around the world and luxury shopping sprees and her father's obsession with investing, all she got was "Devil Nanny's" halfway smiles and side hugs. Angela learned very early that she was on her own, and she had to make do for herself. She taught herself pretty much everything, from how to wear a tampon to how to help her first boyfriend put on his condom. She also learned how to get the attention she desperately wanted from other places, especially the opposite sex. One day in sixth grade, while Angela was walking to class, a group of boys whistled and blew kisses at her, screaming, "Sexy mama! Ooh, baby, you so fine!" That was the beginning of her promiscuity and the end of her chasing after her parents' affection.

Angela learned that what she couldn't get at home, she could get out in the world. Angela's name was a regular on the circuit; she was known for her good looks and beautiful hair. Every boy wanted her, and every girl wanted to be her. She was, of course, the most popular girl at her high school. Angela was a force to be reckoned with, and she was not only popular but also a leader. Her presence commanded attention, and all the boys knew she was secretly down to make out after school behind the bleachers.

When Angela was in the tenth grade, her father came home early from a business trip and caught her in bed with Nathan Cats, the sophomore class president. Angela and Nathan had only been dating for three weeks when she decided she was tired of spending her days at home alone and invited him over for a movie and snacks, which led to an intense makeout session. Angela decided to risk it all on Nathan since he was smart, handsome, and well off. Even though she and Nathan had no idea what they were doing, it felt like the moment. With no protection and no experience, they decided to give "doing it" a try. Kissing led to touching, which led to undressing, which led to skin-on-skin rubbing.

Just when things were about to take a turn towards the irreversible, Angela's dad burst into her room, yelling, "What the hell are you doing, Angie?!" Nathan, without hesitation, jumped up and stood face-to-face with Leeland. His anatomy was full, and he was embarrassed.

"You got two seconds before I get my shotgun!"

Nathan grabbed his things and ran all the way home. In that moment, Leeland realized he had failed his daughter, and this was his fault. He couldn't even be mad; he just told her to get dressed and invited her to the kitchen for tea and conversation!

At sixteen, Angela became pregnant with Nathan's baby, and her mother forced her to get an abortion, so out of sheer spite, she became pregnant again with Nathan. This time, she didn't tell anyone, not even Nathan. She broke up with him and begged him to leave her alone. She went on to hide her pregnancy as long as she could. When her parents learned she was pregnant again and was too far along to abort, they organized an adoption. Angela had no choice in the matter; she was sent away to a special school for wealthy pregnant girls. She gave birth to a baby girl that she didn't even get to hold. As soon as she came out of the womb, doctors whisked her away at the request of her parents.

"Angela, it's easier this way. If you see the baby, then you will want to keep it."

The only thing she had to remember her baby by was the sound of her cries. At that moment, she decided to never return to her parents. When her studies were complete at the girls' school, she went directly to college at Spelman and then to law school. She shunned her parents and refused any of their financial help. She's only seen them once at her graduation from law school, which was ten years ago. She never talks to them on the phone and refuses their calls. Given her history, she vowed to never mistreat a child or refuse help to a child who was in need. Naturally, when she met Otis's baby cousin Jaines, it was love at first sight.

When Angela arrived at the hospital, Jaines was in ICU and unable to be visited by anyone. Doctors were still trying to stabilize her.

"Baby, what's going on? What happened to her?"

Otis was sitting in the ICU waiting room with a face of sheer trepidation. Angela had never seen him look so scared.

Angela sat next to Otis and kissed his cheek and squeezed his hand.

"I know this is hard for you, baby, but can you please try to tell me what's going on?"

Otis kept his head down and mumbled, "Suicide."

"What, baby?"

"Suicide, Ang! She tried to commit suicide!"

"Oh, shit!"

Angela couldn't believe what she was hearing. As she sat back in her chair with the back of her head against the wall, tears began to flood down her face. Her sweet little Jaines didn't want to be alive anymore? But why? Didn't she have the best life, with the two best big cousins ever? What the hell was happening? Angela was so lost and confused. She had so many questions, but she knew it was not the time to ask.

"Mr. and Mrs. McGee, we have some news on Leola's condition."

Dr. Tall, Dark, and Handsome was approaching with a grim look on his face. Angela shot up out of her seat to greet him.

"She is currently stable; however, she is fighting for her life. Leola ingested several high-potency narcotics that are known to cause an overdose. She has a mixture of oxycodone and xanax in her system. She is currently in a coma."

Angela's knees buckled, and she started to go down. Otis quickly grabbed her and led her to a chair.

"Will she survive, sir?" Otis asked with tears streaming down his face.

"Right now, we just have to wait and see. We don't have a prognosis at this time; however, her brain activity is good. By tomorrow morning, we should be able to see if she is out of the woods."

Dr. Tall, Dark, and Handsome shook his head, said, "She is lucky to be alive," and walked away.

"Otis, please help me understand why Jaines would want to kill herself. Baby, why would she do this?"

Just as Otis was about answer Angela, Jaines's mother burst into the waiting room in a rage. "Otis, what the fuck you do to my daughter, huh? I knew I couldn't trust you with her! What the fuck you do to her, huh? You been touching on her like you did me? Is that it?"

Angela's head was spinning. What was she hearing? *Otis touching ... Wait, he touched who?*

It was silent. Everyone stood still. Angela, Otis, and Lainey stood staring at each other face to face. Lainey looked Angela in the eye with a sly smirk and said, "You think you know him, huh, bitch? But you don't know nothing!"

FIVE

"It's all a blur. I don't remember what happened."

Jaines was slowly coming back to herself. It had been two weeks since her suicide attempt, and today, she had been fully awake for a two hours when the social worker came in and began asking her questions.

Jaines was struggling to speak, her voice was low and raspy, and her memory was foggy. She was still in ICU and unable to eat solid foods. However, she was no longer in the "dead zone." She was surely going to live, though the quality of life she would have was yet to be seen. Lainey was not allowed to stay in the room with Jaines; she was kicked out of the hospital for being under the influence of something the last time she visited. Maybe she was just intoxicated with anger and rage. So far, the only ones allowed in the room are Angela and Otis since they are her legal guardians. The doctors, social workers, police, and physical therapists had been in and out of the room all day long asking Angela and Otis many questions.

"You touched her, didn't you?" Angela kept hearing Lainey's voice in her head over and over again. Now, everyone knew Lainey was a few chickens short of a full coop. But it was something in her tone and her eyes that shook Angela's soul. She couldn't let it go.

Lainey said I don't know O, huh? Angela thought to herself as she sat in a daze beside Jaines's bed.

Her thoughts had been spiraling out of control. *I been known O! Hell, for fifteen years, my essence has had him in a trance. If anybody knows him, I know him. What the hell did Lainey mean? Was she high? She has a history of being a crackhead, but she looked healthy, and she's been involved with Jaines more often than not lately, so I don't think she's using right now.*

"What the hell, man?" she said softly to herself before retreating back to her thoughts.

I have to figure out what's going on Otis had been avoiding Angela like the plague since everything happened. He wouldn't even look her in the eyes.

Maybe Lainey was right. Maybe Angela really didn't know her husband.

"Baby, come on. You've been in here all night. We need to go get something to eat or some fresh air."

Otis was standing next to Angela in the hospital room.

"I'm not hungry. I can't eat right now," said Angela.

An awkward silence ensued, then suddenly, Angela looking and looked Otis square in the eyes.

With a soft voice, she almost whispered, "Baby, have you been touching on Jaines? What was Lainey talking about? Why would Jaines do this to herself?" she said as she searched his face, trying to discern his response.

Otis was stunned. He grabbed Angela softly by her shoulders and pulled her in close. "Baby, Lainey is a lying crackhead ass bitch. You can't believe nothing she says. Hell, no. I would never hurt Jaines like that."

Otis released Angela from his embrace. With his hands still on her shoulders, he stepped back and looked in her eyes. "Look at me, baby. I would never lie to you. I love Jaines. Do you believe me?"

Angela did not know who was more convincing, but right now, it was all too much. She just wanted to focus on getting her little cousin out of this place. However, she wasn't done finding out who was telling the truth. This was only the beginning.

Otis and Angela were sitting in a meeting with Jaines's medical team, discussing her current state and her outlook. Angela was becoming more and more frustrated by the minute. She couldn't stop looking Otis upside his head, trying to figure out why he was acting so weird or why Lainey would say what she said.

"Excuse me, I need to use the restroom. I'll be right back."

Running past the restroom, she stopped by Jaines's room to grab her keys and bag as she hurriedly walked to her car. *If I can get to the house, maybe I can find something that will help me understand why Jaines would do this*, Angela thought as she sped down the highway towards her gated community in the Hills.

She swiftly pulled into her garage and ran into her house and up the stairs to Jaines's room. She rummaged through her dressers, looking for anything she could find. She was hoping she'd find some condoms, because then, maybe, Jaines was heartbroken over some young fool who filled her head with lies. She quickly shifted her focus to finding her cell phone.

"Aha! That's it! Where's that damn phone? Teenagers keep everything in their phones," Angela said, talking out loud to herself as she ransacked Jaines's room looking for any little piece of evidence she could find.

After thirty minutes of frantically searching, Angela was heated with frustration. Just as she was about to give up, she saw a shiny silver lock hanging from the edge of Jaines's mattress. Angela quickly lifted the California King-sized mattress, and to her surprise!!!

"Her DIARY!!" Angela yelled as she grabbed the diary and jumped up and down like a kid at Disney World. "All the answers I need are right in this book. I can feel it!"

But damn. I don't have the key. Angela immediately began another rampage in the room searching for the key. After an hour of searching and ten missed calls from Otis, Angela finally flopped down on the floor in defeat. With tears rolling down her face, she began to pray a silent prayer to God.

"Dear God, I know something is off here, and maybe I have been oblivious this entire time. Father, forgive me for not seeing that my cousin needed me in ways she couldn't express. God, please, I pray You help me find out what led Jaines to try to kill herself. Please heal her mind, body, and soul. And give me the knowledge to uncover the truth, the power to prosecute whoever is at fault, and the strength to handle what I am about to find out! Amen."

"Ugh!" she screamed as she used all of her might to pull both sides of the diary in opposite directions in an attempt to break it open.

"Yes!!" she yelled in excitement, tears still rolling down her face as she finally opened the book and frantically searched through the pages for answers.

"Blank. Why are all of the pages blank? What the hell is this?" she said aloud in frustration at the emptiness of Jaines's diary, wondering why nothing was there.

"Hello," she finally answered Otis's call.

"Baby, where are you? The medical team couldn't move forward without your signatures!" Otis exclaimed.

"Oh. I'm sorry, this is all too much for me. I needed a break," she said, exasperated.

"I know, baby, but please get back here. We have to make some decisions," Otis expressed.

"I'm on my way." Angela ended the call as she prepared to head out the door and back to the hospital.

Ding! Dong! Ding!

The doorbell rang so loudly and suddenly that Angela jumped from fear. She gathered herself and ran down the stairs to the door and flung it open in a panic, not knowing who it could possibly be.

"Oh! I'm sorry, Mrs. McGee. I didn't mean to scare you." It was Jaines's best friend.

"Elizaveth!! Oh! Hi, baby!"

From the look on her face, she was scared, so Angela gave her a hug. Elizaveth melted into Angela's bosom and began to sob uncontrollably.

Angela was overwhelmed. "Baby, don't cry. Everything

is going to be okay, I promise. Jaines is doing better and will be home soon, sweetie.”

“She is my best friend. I can’t lose her,” Elizaveth cried.

“It’s okay. Come inside so we can talk.”

Once inside, Angela made Elizaveth some warm chamomile tea to calm her nerves. She knew she had to get back to the hospital, but she also knew Elizaveth could be the key to cracking this case. Once settled, Elizaveth started talking nonstop, like word vomit. She told Angela that a few weeks before the incident, Otis made Jaines quit the cheer team abruptly with no explanation, and that whenever she was away, Otis would take Jaines’s phone and would not allow her to use it until he knew Angela was coming back. Elizaveth told Angela that Jaines was scared of Otis sometimes because he wanted to control her every move.

“Miss Angela, I need to tell you something that Jaines promised me not to tell anyone.”

Elizaveth was looking Angela directly in the eyes with fear and apprehension.

“Tell me, sweetie, please,” Angela begged Elizaveth.

“Well,” said Elizaveth, “Jaines told me that, um …” She paused to take a deep breath and clear her throat, then continued. “One day, she said that she and, uh … I mean, I don’t know if it’s true, but …”

Just as she was about to spill it, the front door burst open!!

“Niña, ven aquí AHORA!!!”

Elizaveth’s mother was in a fit. “What are you doing here, niña? haven’t I told you to stay away from this house?!”

“Wait, what’s going on? She is just worried about Jaines.

Wait a minute—why don't you want her here?"

Angela was in shock at the disdain being shown by Elizaveth's mother.

"My daughter knows better than to come here. I'm sorry about your little cousin, but she can no longer be friends with my daughter!" Elizaveth's mother grabbed her daughter's arm and dragged her out the front door, but not without Elizaveth leaving Angela one last clue before she left.

Elizaveth, who was crying and screaming as she was being dragged away, managed to scream out, "Angela, please believe me, it's Oti—!"

"Callete! Ya has dicho suficiente!" yelled Elizaveth's mother as she threw her into the car and sped away.

"Shut up! You have said enough!" Angela knew what Elizaveth's mother was saying. Given the line of work she was in, it was important for her to be fluent in at least two other languages, and Spanish just happened to be one, French being the other. Angela was in a whirlwind, and she became dizzy and faint. She raced to the restroom to splash cold water on her face. Looking at her reflection in the mirror, she knew she had to tighten up if she was going to get to the bottom of this one.

"Hello?"

"Yeah, Peter? It's me, Angela."

"Oh, hey, Ang. How's Jaines? Is she all right?"

"She's doing better. Hey, listen, I need you to run a quick background on someone for me."

"Cool. Shoot me the details."

"His name is Otis McGee."

"Okay. Otis McG—wait, isn't that your husband's name?"

"Yeah, run it! And tell me everything you find!"

SIX

Otis Mac McGee was born on July 4, 1981, to Jacob and Nellie McGee. Otis was the baby of six boys. Nellie thought she was cursed for having a boy six times: "God don't favor my prayers; I got all these sons, not one girl."

Her overall disposition was mean, tired, and angry with a hint of softness every now and then when she had the energy. Otis's dad worked a full-time job at the steel mill down the road in Chicago, where he eventually retired. He made enough money for their mother to stay home and take care of the house and kids and still take at least one family vacation a year. Otis, since he was the baby of the family, was everyone's favorite. The apple of his father's eye. His father always said, "We got it wrong five times, but we got it right with you. You gon' be somebody."

Otis never understood why his father favored him, but he liked it, so he never questioned it. Although Otis was loved and favored by his father, he was hated and envied by his brothers. Otis's brothers ranged in age from nine to twenty-four years old. LeeRay was his oldest brother; he was never home. He was a gigolo who traveled back and forth from woman to woman. He wasn't a problem for Otis; it was his other brothers, the ones who lived in the house on a daily basis, who hated him and made his life miserable every single chance they got. One day, Otis came home from school with a busted lip, and his father flew into a rage. "What the hell happened to my boy?" He was yelling and demanding answers from everyone, even the walls in the house!

"Daddy, Otis was being messed with by a bully, but we got him off of him." Jessie, Otis's third oldest brother, was lying. He was the bully, and he did not get off of him. Jessie was mad at Otis because he got an A in math, and he knew he would get a present when he got home. See, Daddy always rewarded the boys with money or candy when they brought home an A. Problem is, they never brought home A's. Except Otis; he always got straight A's and had perfect attendance.

"You make me sick. You think you better than all of us, huh? his big brother, Jessie, yelled.

"No, I don't, honest. I just get good grades in math is all."

"Nah, you always trying to outdo us!" Jessie was raging with heat as he and his brothers walked home from school. He was so jealous of Otis that he tripped him from behind, and when Otis fell, he laughed and started kicking him. In a fit of rage and anger, their other four brothers joined in, all stomping Otis until the oldest made them stop.

"All right, that's enough. The little punk can't take much more."

"I'm going to tell Daddy when I get home! He gon' get all of y'all!" Otis screamed as he got up and dusted himself off.

"You ain't gon' be able to tell nobody nothing if your lip

is busted, little punk!" Just then, Jessie cocked his arm back and punched Otis hard, square in the mouth!

"OOOH!" yelled his other brothers as they watched.

Otis was hurt bad; his lip was bleeding, and he could feel a tooth floating around in his mouth. His brother hit him so hard it knocked him right off his feet onto his bottom. Otis was spitting blood from his front tooth being knocked out. Now, at the time, Otis was only seven-and-a-half years old and weighed about forty-five pounds soaking wet. It was an unfair deal that Otis didn't deserve. But he learned something in that moment: Even as a seven-year-old boy, he knew he would be hated for his greatness for the rest of his life. He knew his brothers only hated him because their father loved him more! He was angry at his father. *Why does he love me more? Why can't he love us all the same?* he thought.

He was angry at his brothers. *Why do they hate me? It's not my fault Daddy loves me more.* He was angry at himself. *Why am I so weak? Why can't I just fight back?*

"I think you knocked his tooth out, man!" one of the brothers shouted. The sound of his voice shook Otis out of his thoughts and back to reality.

"Ah, he'll be fine. We'll just say he got beat up by a bully."

Jessie led the crew of brothers back to the house with their lie intact. Otis cried the whole way home. It was that very day that he realized he could never trust his brothers again, and he hardened his heart towards them. Once the boys reached the house, Daddy was heated. When Daddy finally calmed down, he and Otis's mom took him into a room by himself and asked him what was going on. But his mouth was swollen, and his lip was busted pretty bad. His daddy examined his face and forced his mouth open. When he saw his tooth was missing, he jumped up and told his wife, "Get the keys. We going to that damn school to find out who the hell this bully is!"

Mama dragged Otis out to the car by the hand as she and Daddy sped away to the school. When they arrived, the principal was just leaving, until Daddy hopped out of the car and yelled, "Hey, you! What kind of principal are you, huh?"

That began the entire unfolding of the lie. After speaking with the principal for about an hour, she and Otis's parents made him write a statement since he couldn't speak. She also told his parents he needed to be taken to the doctor and dentist immediately, which they knew. In his statement, Otis told the entire truth and implicated each one of his brothers. The principal read the statement out loud to Otis's parents:

"Today, we were walking home from school, and Jessie tripped me from behind because I got an A in math again. Then, he and the rest of my brothers stomped me until I couldn't take anymore. When I got up, I told them I was going to tell my daddy; that's when Jessie busted me in the mouth and said I can't tell nobody if I got a busted lip. There is no bully besides my brothers. They hate me. They torture me because my daddy loves me more."

Hearing the truth was all too much for Otis's parents. They apologized for taking the principal's time and accusing her of being incompetent. Daddy was so mad he couldn't speak; he actually dropped his head and cried. This was the first time Otis had ever seen his daddy cry, and it scared him. His mother kept her cool and led them to the car.

As soon as they left, the principal contacted Child Protective Services, gave them Otis's statement, and claimed she was concerned about his safety.

At the hospital, the doctors noticed many old marks and bruises and some fresh ones from the stomping Otis endured earlier. They asked his parents about them, but they had no idea he had them. Back in the doctors' quarters, they were planning to file a report to Child Protective Services, given the nature of the bruises and old scars found on Otis's body.

"Nellie, I can't go back home to the boys tonight. If I do, I might kill them. I am going to drop you off, and I am taking Otis with me," Jacob insisted to Nellie.

"When you get home, clean up real good and make the house nice and neat. It's a storm coming. The white folk gon' try to take my boy from me. I can feel it."

"Honey, everything is going to be fine. They don't have no reason to come for Otis."

"Woman, you must be crazy! The boy is all bruised up, and his brother knocked his tooth out. He's not safe in his own house. Hell, if I can see it, they can too." His father was steaming with frustration that Nellie would not accept the truth.

"All them other sons of mine is rotten, no good for nothing. I'd give 'em all away if I could. Tell them when I return they gon' have hell to pay."

It was a quiet ride home as Jacob dropped off Nellie, and he and Otis sped away to his brother's house. Three days later, Otis was called out of class to go down to the counselor's office. When he arrived, he was greeted by a white lady with long, stringy grey hair in a blue pinstriped suit.

"Otis, this is Mrs. Roberson. She works with the department of Child Protective Services. She just wanted to ask you a few questions about the incident the other day."

Otis had just returned to school after recovering from the fight with his brothers. He still had five stitches in his lip that hadn't dissolved yet, and his new fake tooth was still settling into its place. He couldn't eat anything fun, no candy, no apples, nothing solid for a week.

"Yes, ma'am," Otis replied.

After about thirty minutes of questioning, he was allowed to go back to class. Since the incident, Otis was no longer allowed to walk home with his brothers; instead, Daddy made his brothers walk while he rode the bus. When Otis got home, there were two police cars and a few other unfamiliar cars in his driveway.

As he approached the porch, his father was being taken away by police. He was handcuffed.

"Daddy, what's going on? Where are they taking you? Daddy, please take me with you!" Otis screamed.

"It's okay, son. Everything will be okay. Mama will take care of you, and I'll be right back, okay?"

Little did Otis know that the day his brothers attacked him would be the day that changed his entire life. The doctors and the school principals both reported Otis's parents to state welfare for children, which led to investigations. That led to them finding out that Otis's brothers had been torturing him secretly for years. The day after the beating, Daddy returned home in a rage and beat all of Otis's brothers with the belt. When the welfare check happened, the investigators saw the fresh welts, but despite Daddy trying to explain why he was so angry and despite all of his apologies, he was arrested for child abuse and neglect. Daddy being arrested was only the beginning of the end of life as Otis knew it.

"Now, boys, don't be afraid, but you will have to go away for just a little bit. I promise Mama and Daddy will get you back really soon."

Nellie was explaining to her boys after sitting them all down in the living room under the watchful eye of Mrs. Roberson, the lady who interviewed Otis at school.

"You will have to stay with some people just for a little while, until we sort this all out, okay?" Mama explained as all the boys wept and cried, screaming and begging to stay at home but to no avail.

At this point, everyone was crying and begging. Even Mama was saying, "Please don't take my babies. They all I got."

"This is all my fault. I'm sorry, Otis! I'm so sorry!" Jessie screamed as the scene became more and more chaotic.

Otis was so confused and did not understand what was happening. All he kept thinking about was his daddy. *Where is he going? Why did the police take him? He was just protecting me.*

"Otis, let's go, sweetheart."

The sound of Mrs. Roberson's voice shook Otis out of his daze. All five boys were being taken from the home and put into separate cars and being driven to different foster homes. The people didn't even look back as Mama was sprawled out on the sidewalk on her belly, kicking and screaming, "Please don't take my babies! Please!"

One of the neighbors came and helped her to feet and back into the house. Nellie had lost it all in one day, her husband and all five of her sons. Mrs. Roberson promised Nellie this was only temporary, and the boys would be returned as soon as they could assure the home was safe.

"The boys all need some therapy to understand the nature of their abuse towards their brother. Once they are clear on how to have appropriate sibling relationships, they can be returned," Mrs. Roberson explained.

All of this had proven to be too much for Otis's mother, and she was hospitalized the same evening due to a nervous breakdown. Otis's daddy was booked, processed, and released the next day on bond, which his brother paid. Upon his release, he found out all his boys had been taken to different homes! In desperation, he cried and begged God for help. All he wanted was Otis, but Otis was on his way to somewhere far from home, a place that would inevitably change the core of his soul forever!

SEVEN

When Otis arrived at his foster home, he was scared and tired from crying for five hours straight. "Otis, I promise you will like it here, and this is only temporary," Mrs. Roberson explained as she tried to console Otis. But he could not be consoled.

"Good evening, Mrs. Roberson," said a tall, lanky man with dark, curly hair and black eyes.

"Good evening, Steven. This is Otis, your new recruit." Both Mrs. Roberson and Steven laughed, but Otis didn't know what was funny.

"Otis is seven-and-a-half years old and the baby of five brothers. He will only be with you temporarily until his family can receive the therapy they need to function like civilized human beings."

"Oh, okay. I see. Another poor, Black, fatherless baby from the ghetto?" the tall lanky man asked sarcastically.

Otis was angry and scared but also paying attention to the conversation. *Ghetto? Poor? Fatherless? Who is he talking about?* he wondered. *And what is a ghetto?*

"Well, actually, this one is quite the contrary, Mr. Reeves.

He has a father and a mother who have done very well by him. He just has some unfortunate misunderstandings with his siblings that need to be sorted out."

"Ah, okay. I see," the man responded.

"Yes, which is why he will be returning home very soon. We thought you would be the best temporary placement for him."

"Okay. Well, little Otis, welcome to Casa Reeves! I'll do the best I can to help you while I have you."

"Otis, you will be pleased to know that Mr. Reeves has two sons of his own that you can play with. Isn't that right, Steven?" the caseworker said in an effort to comfort Otis.

"Yep, and they are in the backyard playing soccer if you want to join them."

Otis shook his head no.

"It may take him a while to warm up, Steven. He has had a very traumatic past couple of days, which is why his therapist will be contacting you to set up a session ASAP."

"Okay. I am no stranger to trauma; I'm sure he will be fine with time."

"Touché. I'll check back with you tomorrow to see how he made it through the night." Mrs. Roberson said her final goodbyes, kissed Otis on his forehead, and assured him he would like it there.

While Otis was scared and angry, he couldn't help but notice how nice Mr. Reeves seemed to be.

"Okay, O—can I call you O? Or would you prefer Otis?" Mr. Reeves asked Otis as he led him to the back yard.

Otis did not respond.

"Okay, little fella. I'll call you O; it's easier to say. Less syllables, you know?"

Once in the backyard, Mr. Reeves introduced Otis to his two sons, one aged nine and one aged eleven. The eleven-year-old was tall and husky and already had a slight mustache, a deep voice, and firm handshake, which intimidated Otis right away. The nine-year-old was more like Mr. Reeves in shape, tall and lanky, with more baby features, definitely no mustache, and a yucky limp handshake. Otis thought he could take him in a fight if he had to. The boys were also kind and took Otis up to their room to help him put away his things and show him where he would be sleeping. Otis was so emotional; he already missed his family and was scared of what would happen to his father. He couldn't stop crying. The boys began to do something Otis had never really seen anyone do. They both came over to him and grabbed his hands and began saying words like "Father God" and "Jesus."

"What are you doing?" Otis asked.

"We are praying to God and Jesus and asking them to put a Band-Aid on your broken heart."

"Who are they?" Otis inquired.

"Wow. You literally don't know God and Jesus? No wonder you're so upset!" said the husky brother as they both laughed in disbelief.

"Mom and Dad will tell you all about them, and trust me, you will be hearing a lot about them at church on Wednesday. Sundays too. Before you leave this place, you will know them really good," said the brothers in unison as they left Otis alone in the room to put away his things.

Later that evening, while at dinner, Otis learned all about

the Reeves and how they are devout Christians who attend church regularly. "Mother Reeves," which he MUST call her, is a nurse practitioner at the local hospital, while "Father Reeves" is the first and only African American train conductor in their city. He is a highly respected man and very well known around these parts. His name and biography have even been added to the local African American History Museum. The brothers are also popular in the affluent crowd and are excelling in athletics at their local private school. Otis also learned where he fit in the perfect circle, and it was nowhere. He didn't fit. In fact, he couldn't wait to go back home to his imperfect life, with his imperfect family and siblings. Where he was known, even if he was misunderstood. Where he was loved by his father.

Otis was well into his first month stay with the Reeves family before he got to have his first supervised visitation with his mother and father. It was an early Sunday morning when Mother Reeves woke Otis up with a surprise announcement.

"Get up, Otis. It's a big day for you! You get to see your ma and pa today."

"Ma and pa? You mean my daddy and mama? I'm gonna see them?"

"Yep! Now, get on up and put on some Sunday clothes so you can look nice when you do!"

After thirty minutes of grooming and getting ready, Otis and Mother Reeves headed out the door for a two-hour trip to Chicago to see Otis's mama and daddy. When they arrived at the visitation center, Otis was so excited that he started to cry out of sheer joy. He hadn't seen or heard from his family in an entire month. He didn't know where any of his brothers were or if his mama and daddy were dead or alive. As far as he knew, his daddy was still in prison for taking the belt to his brothers.

After being processed into the visitation center, Mother Reeves told Otis she would be back in about an hour and a half to pick him up and take him back with her, so he shouldn't get too excited about seeing his parents because he still wasn't allowed to leave with them. But Otis didn't care what she said, and he had made up his mind. He was going to let his heart be as excited as it could be. After Mother Reeves left, Otis was led down a long white hallway into a huge room with glass windows. It looked like what he imagined a prison cell to look like. When he entered the room, he saw it was laid out with a sofa, a television, some books, board games, and toys. He also noticed a huge digital clock right above the door that said *Time Remaining 1:30*, and it was already winding down.

"Your mother and father will be right in," he was told by the escort coldly as she swiftly walked out and slammed the door.

"Wait, shouldn't my time start when they get here?"

But there was no one there to answer him. About five minutes later, he could hear the door handle jingle and saw the door fly open!

"Otis!! My boy!"

Otis ran to his father and jumped in his arms. He held on for dear life. He squeezed so hard he thought he would break him.

"Daddy!" Otis cried huge tears, and he screamed, "Daddy! Daddy!" over and over again. He hugged him so tight and kept sniffing his neck. He missed his father's scent.

"Otis, my boy. I missed you so much, son. I'm fighting to get you home, son."

"Daddy, please take me with you! Please, Daddy!"

"It's okay, son. I promise Daddy's gon' get you home soon."

"Okay." Otis sobbed as he was still wrapped up in his father's arms with his face buried in his neck.

"Where's Mama?" Otis managed to ask through his tears.

"I need to talk to you about that, son, but right now I just wanna hold ya for a little while longer."

After silently hugging and sniffing his daddy's neck, Otis finally calmed down enough to loosen his embrace. But his father didn't rush him; he just let him hold him as long as he wanted. Once Otis loosened his grip, his father sat him down in front of the board games. He started unboxing one and taking out the pieces. He figured he'd play a little game with him and try his best to distract him from the bad news he had about his mother and brothers.

"Daddy, where is Mama? How come she didn't come see me too?" Otis asked as he rolled the dice and moved his thimble six spaces to the left.

"Well, son, see, that's the thing. Um … ya mama … Well, she … You see, she is…"

Otis could see his father was struggling to speak and not making eye contact. Then, his dad took a big, deep breath, and tears welled up in his eyes. This was only the second time he'd ever seen his father cry.

"You see, your mama … Well, she was upset pretty bad when she had her whole life taken away from her right before her eyes. She was so sick. She had an episode and was hospitalized. She hasn't been the same ever since, son."

"Where is she?" Otis asked with tears in his eyes as his heart was breaking.

"Son, she is in a special place for people like her who need 'round-the-clock care. We are trying to get her back to herself again so we can all be reunited. But for now, what she needs is more than I can provide for her on my own."

"This is all my fault, Daddy. If I had never told on my brothers, Mama would be okay, and I could be home with you! I just wanna go home. I just want Mama!" Otis cried.

His father was overwhelmed that his boy was so hurt but had no words to comfort him. He just scooped him up in his arms and rocked him until he fell asleep. He looked at the clock; there were only twenty minutes left. He couldn't believe an hour and ten minutes had already gone by. He was devastated that he was about to have to leave his boy in this state. He couldn't imagine not being able to take his own son home with him. He wondered how he got to this place in his life where he couldn't take control of something that was solely his! This was his boy, with his DNA in his blood! He named him, he fed him, he raised him. He was his and his alone. He wasn't about to let the white folks tell him no more how to raise his own son. Right then, Jacob decided that the white folk had done enough.

"They done took all my boys, drove my Nellie insane, and now they ain't gone let me leave with my own child," he said to himself. "Ain't letting 'em take nothing else that belong to me."

Jacob knocked on the glass to get the attention of the worker sitting behind it who was supervising their visit.

"Hey. My boy is sleeping, but I want to take him to the snack parlor before I leave," Jacob told the young male worker.

"That's fine. The snack parlor is down the hall to the left. Just tap the glass when you return, and I will let you back in."

"Can I take him with me?" Jacob asked, pretending to be compliant, knowing he was going to take him despite what the worker had to say. And he was prepared to fight if he had to.

"Sure, you can. We usually don't allow it, but I've heard nothing but good things about you, so I'm sure it's fine."

"Okay. Thank you, sir," Jacob replied as he walked out the door, relieved that he didn't have to cold cock the young man for only trying to do his job. He walked quickly down the hall past the snack parlor, straight to the back of the building and out of the back door with his son in his arms. As soon as he was outside, he ran to his car as fast as he could, strapped Otis in, and sped off into the sunset. He couldn't believe he just had to kidnap his own son, and he knew nobody would understand. But he wouldn't be able to live with himself if he had to watch his boy beg and scream to come with him, only to walk away and leave him! He didn't know where he was going to go, or how long it would be until the white folks would be on his tail, but one thing he did know was that he wasn't going down without a fight. He would be willing to die to hold on to any part of the life he once lived, and Otis was the only part of that life he had left!

When Otis woke up, he realized immediately that he was still with his father.

"Daddy, did you steal me back?" Otis asked with fear and

excitement. He felt excited to be with his daddy, but fearful of what might happen if anyone found out.

"Listen, O, you can't tell nobody what's going on, okay? We gotta play it cool, son. I'm not gon' let nobody else take you from me ever again," Jacob told Otis with sincere certainty, knowing he would be willing to die to keep his son.

"But where we going, Daddy? Where are my brothers? Can we steal them back too?" Otis asked.

"Your brothers is rotten, and we wouldn't even be in this if it wasn't for them. Forget about them. From here on out, it's just me and you, son," Jacob replied as he sped down the highway, headed towards his brother's house out in the country of Chicago, Illinois. He hoped his brother would take them in and hide them until he could figure out his next move.

"Okay, Daddy," Otis said, knowing he was safe now; knowing that his dad would die for him.

Knowing he was his father's favorite. Knowing his father would protect him from his brothers and from people like the Reeves. Knowing his nightmare was finally over!

Otis and his dad drove through the night to his uncle's house in the countryside of Chicago.

When Mrs. Reeves went back to retrieve Otis from his visit, she was greeted by the police and Otis's caseworker. "Mrs. Reeves, we are sorry to inform you that Otis was taken from the visit by his father."

Mrs. Reeves felt a bit at ease knowing that Otis was back with his father; after all, he was so miserable with her and her family the last month. Not to mention the thing that happened with her and her boys that one weekend, which she made Otis promise to keep a secret forever and ever.

"Honestly, I think he is better off with his father. He was only one more visit away from going back home," Mrs. Reeves argued in Jacob's favor.

"Otis was not thriving in our home. The grief of him being away from his father was becoming too much for him. I really think we should just let it all be. It's for the best."

After careful deliberations with law enforcement and child welfare officials, everyone decided that Otis would be allowed to stay with his father. His caseworker took on the task of locating them and informing them they no longer had to live in fear and that Otis was cleared to be in his father's legal custody again.

After trying for three weeks, the caseworker was able to locate Jacob and tell him that their board decided to award him sole custody of Otis since he had worked his program and completed all of his therapy. He was granted leniency for taking Otis from his last visit due what was called a "miscommunication" in protocol. Jacob and Otis were free. Under one condition.

Otis's uncle had to pass a home visit, and Otis had to complete six months of reunification therapy with his father before his case was completely closed. Jacob's brother was able to pass his home visit with no issue, and due to the amount of space on his farm, Jacob was also offered the choice to take in his five other sons. But Jacob declined, stating Otis would not be safe and that he was not financially able to care for six boys on his own. Otis's other brothers were released from foster care and dispersed to aunts and uncles within the family.

While his mother remained under the guardianship of the local state hospital, Otis lived with his father and tried to recover from his time in foster care with the Reeves. A time in his life that changed the very core of Otis's soul and the course of his life forever!

EIGHT

Jaines was waking up and becoming more coherent every day. She was slowly starting to remember who she was and where she was, but the details of what happened to her were still a blur. However, she was released from the hospital two weeks after she woke up from her coma. Now, she has an in-home attendant who provides health care services to her around the clock while Angela and Otis are away at work. Jaines is doing much better; physically, she expressed no limitations. However, cognitively, she is struggling but slowly getting back to her old self. Since she has been home, she has been having regular visits from school friends who bring her work and help her complete whatever she can just to maintain some social aspect of life.

Today, Jaines was working on her algebra test with her classmate, the cutie she bumped into in the hallway. "Jaines, hey, do you understand this stuff?"

"Mm-hmm." She shook her head up and down. "Please Excuse My Dear Aunt Sally. That's how I remember what to do with the exponents and stuff."

"Jaines, everyone at school has been worried and wondering

what happened to you."

"I tried to kill myself; that's what happened. I'm sure you heard."

"I mean, yeah, we all heard, but why? Look at your life. It's literally perfect. Everyone wants to be you, and every guy wants to date you."

"Every guy?" Jaines asked as she looked into his eyes with sweet, innocent expectation.

"Yeah, every guy." He smiled and looking back at her. They sat gazing at each other for what felt like forever before his phone vibrated and scared them both back to reality.

"Look, J, it's no secret I like you. Why you think I volunteered to help you with your work every Tuesday and Thursday? Definitely not because I like algebra."

They both laughed.

Jaines ignored that he said he liked her; she was so confused about life at the moment that the last thing she needed was for a boy to add to that confusion. She skated right past the comment and went back to the initial question.

"I tried to kill myself because I do not live the perfect life. I hate my life. It looks pretty on the outside, but it's ugly inside, just like me."

"J, you're the most beautiful girl I know, inside and out," Andre expressed.

"Really?" Jaines was laying down in her bed, with Andre sitting in a study chair beside her, as she abruptly sat up in frustration.

"If I am so beautiful, then why did my father abandon

me?! Huh? Why have I never met him? Why did my own mother beat the shit out of me for the smallest things? Huh? If I'm so beautiful, then why did my only hope die and leave me with this monster of a man? If I'm *so damn* beautiful, then why does my cousin violate me every chance he gets?!

Before she could stop the word vomit, it was too late. She had said too much. It was out now, and she could not take it back. He was only the second person she had ever told besides her best friend, Elizaveth.

He sat, shocked and stunned at what he was hearing. Here she was, his crush, the most beautiful girl in his life, the girl he had hoped to take to prom, kiss, and marry one day. She was a beautiful disaster. He stared into her face and was heartbroken at her pain. He slowly moved next to her on the bed and wrapped her in his arms, holding her as tight as he could for as long as she needed. He didn't say a word as they sat in quiet disbelief.

Jaines was scared now; she had told someone she didn't know if she could trust. *What if he tells someone else?* Then her life would be worse than it already was.

As he gathered his things and prepared to leave, he looked back at Jaines and said, "J, I am so sorry for everything you have gone through, but it's not because of you. It's the people around you. You really are beautiful, and you deserve the best life, not this. I promise your business is safe with me."

He hugged her once more and softly kissed her forehead before he left.

For the first time in her life, Jaines felt something in her loins that was not forced by her cousin, and it felt good. She liked it but was afraid and confused by it too.

Oh, my God, do I have a crush? Could I be falling for him? she asked herself as she got back into bed and let thoughts of him carry her to sleep.

As he walked home, Andre's mind rattled with fear and concern for Jaines, and he thought, *I have to get her out of that house.*

Later, around midnight, Janes was awakened by a text from Andre:

I'm outside.

What? Why? she replied.

Listen. If you want to leave, this is our only chance! Andre pleaded.

Otis is gone. I saw his car leave, J! he texted her back to back with urgency.

Where are we going? Jaines inquired.

Anywhere but here, J. I can't let you stay here!

I'm scared, she insisted.

Me too, but this is our only chance, J! Andre was desperate to help her and thought this was the only way.

I'm on my way.

Jaines, in haste, decided to go with Andre, who she'd really just gotten to know a bit better. But she figured she'd rather take her chances with the beautiful stranger than stay there with an all-too-familiar oppressor.

It was now or never. She had to make her move. Jaines quickly and silently grabbed her backpack and her cell phone, stuffing her bag with whatever she could as fast as she could. She looked around her room one last time and shed one single tear. It was the first time in years she actually let a tear fall from her eye. She knew life from this point would never be the same. She was daring to take control of her own destiny. Daring to say, "FUCK YOU!" to Otis. Daring to escape the hell she had been predestined to. Her single tear wasn't for all of the hurt her cousin had caused her; she had no tears left for him. Her tears were for Angela. Her only hope. The only reason she didn't give suicide a round two. Angela was the light in her darkness, but the darkness was too great! It was time to get out before it totally consumed her!

NINE

Angela was away on business in California when she got the call she had been waiting for. It was her friend, Peter, with the results of the background check on Otis.

"Ang, I got something for ya. But you may not like it."

"I'm a big girl, Peter. Shoot it to me straight."

"Your husband's record is as clean as a baby's bottom! Man has never hurt a fly."

"Okay, thanks, Peter. I'll get back with you later!"

"Okay, but wh—"

Click! Angela hung up and exhaled a sigh of relief, happy to know that her beloved husband was not some weird pedophile. *I mean, I have expert knowledge in finding out the truth. I think I'd know if my own husband was a creep, right?* she thought.

But was she right? She couldn't shake her intuition. And she kept hearing Lainey's voice: "You been touching on her too." Her gut was telling her something more was lying right underneath the surface of all of this drama with Jaines. She never knew Jaines to keep a secret from her or tell a lie. But something was off if she tried to commit suicide. Not to mention that Otis had been a totally different human being since it all happened. Something just wasn't right. And she had to find out.

Angela was stumped because Jaines wasn't talking and Elizaveths mother had banned the poor girl from even walking down their street. Jaines had no other friends!

"Aa! That's it!"

And with one phone call, Angela finally found the piece she thought she needed to crack the code!

Ring, ring, ring.

"Peter speaking."

"Peter, I need cell phone records. I need everything. Voicemails, texts, call logs, everything!" Angela said.

"Cool. Shoot me the name and number."

"Jaines McGee. (901) 712-8790."

"Wait, isn't that yo—"

"Listen, Peter, just run the number and give me E-VER-Y-THING! I'll explain later!"

Click.

Peter got right on it. He had been working with Angela as her silent FBI partner for over a decade, and he knew she meant business. He learned firsthand when she represented him back in college and was able to get him off with a petty misdemeanor and seal his records for selling marijuana. He knew that if she needed anything, it was for good reason, which is why he often broke the code for her and pulled records without warrants or any explanation. Angela was safe to work with; she never bent the rules of the game, never revealed her hand too soon. Most importantly, she never gave up her sources.

"Hey, baby. How's your day going?" Angela softly asked Otis, who was on the other line.

"It's good. I just tucked Jaines in. I'm headed to bed myself."

Otis was lying. He didn't tuck Jaines in. He didn't even know Jaines was gone. He wasn't in bed; he was on his way somewhere. Somewhere Angela had no idea about.

Angela thought it was weird that he said he had just tucked Jaines in. Why would he need to tuck in a fifteen-year-old? But she let it slide for the moment.

"Okay, O. I'll give you a call in the morning I before I board. I love you."

"Yes, baby, call me before you board. I love you too. Goodnight."

After hanging up, Angela thought to call Jaines to verify Otis's story since it sounded like he was driving, but he had never had a lying problem before. Or had he? Everything was starting to confuse her, and nobody was who they were before Jaines tried to kill herself. Angela felt like her life had become the twilight zone. She tried calling Jaines twice and was sent to voicemail each time. Maybe she really was asleep! Angela was a ball of nerves; she couldn't settle down. She wanted those phone records. She wanted the truth. She spent the rest of the evening closing out cases and preparing to fly back home. As she began to pack her suitcase for her early flight the next day, her phone rang. It was Peter!

"Check your email, Angela. I sent you everything I could find! Hope it helps."

"Peter, thank you so much. I have a terrible feeling that it will!"

Click.

Angela was afraid to open her email and view the logs. She could feel in her soul that from this moment forward, her life would never be the same. But she could not have prepared herself for what she found. Nothing in this world could have prepared her for it. Death would have been easier!

TEN

Otis was overwhelmed with the weight of his lies and deceit and no longer wanted to hide his truths. But he knew the world wasn't ready for who he really was. He knew he would lose everything if he told anyone about what he was doing to Jaines. He knew it was wrong. But he couldn't help himself. He couldn't stop. Even with the late-night private intense therapy sessions he was having, he couldn't fight the urge to do things he shouldn't do. His brain was rattling with thoughts as he headed to his final therapy session. Since the suicide incident, Otis was remorseful for his actions and decided to get help to find out why he was the way he was. It was like he didn't really understand the gravity of his behavior and how it was affecting Jaines to the point of suicide.

From the moment he saw her lying in the hospital, fighting to live, he knew it was his fault. It was the first time he felt any ounce of sadness or sense of wrongdoing. If she had died, he wouldn't have been able to live with himself. He loved Jaines. She was the closest thing to a daughter he would ever have, since there was no way he would ever have a child with his workaholic wife who had severe mommy and daddy issues and an insatiable desire to rescue every vulnerable person in the world.

Jaines was the only thing that made him feel seen and worthy. He was a Fortune 500 man, the wealthiest his family had ever seen. He alone broke centuries of generational poverty. He was desired by every woman near and far. Every man wanted to be him, and every woman wanted to sleep with him. But he knew it was just his status, only his power they desired. Not his heart. He had the world in his hands, but he felt inadequate and sick, like his soul was the devil's, like he never had a chance. Everything he had ever worked for meant nothing. He could feel the walls closing in on him. He knew his wife was working this thing in secret; she loved Jaines too much to let this go. He knew she would find out, and he was scared. She was a beast. She would have his head. He had to figure out a plan before all of his darkness came to light. He had already destroyed any written evidence of his guilt. Jaines's diary, as far as he knew, was gone; he had landscaped it along with any of her underwear that may have had his DNA on it.

Since the suicide attempt, he had stopped "tucking her in." He knew that was the final straw and that his little cousin couldn't take any more of his hands on her body. Fear of losing her was the only thing that seemed to control his urges.

"Come on in, Mr. McGee. It's nice to see you this evening," said Otis's therapist, an older man by the name of Charles Blythe.

Charles had been in private practice for three decades and had dealt with every facet of demons; nothing was a shock to him. But this was the first time he had ever been offered twenty thousand dollars for six intense private late-night sessions. Twenty thousand dollars to keep it private, even under oath or subpoena, late-night so his client would feel comfortable and maintain a low profile.

At first, it seemed like the deal of a lifetime. After all, what could possibly be eating this man so much? Dr. Blythe thought Otis would be easy money in the bank. However, in Otis's case, he had never come across an individual he felt sorrier for, who left even him conflicted about his integrity as a doctor and a man. Dr. Blythe was constantly thinking about Otis's case; was he evil, or misunderstood? Was he a monster, or just a grown, scared little boy who needed help to tackle his demons? How could he help such an individual? Dr. Blythe knew he had his work cut out for him. And Otis's reputation preceded him. Dr. Blythe could see his prestige and that he was so well wrapped externally, but he was slowly learning that Otis was a dark and tormented soul internally. But it wasn't his job to judge him. No. His only plight was to help Otis understand himself and unpack the trauma that led him to be the man he had become.

"Another late-night session with the doc," Otis said as he adjusted in his seat.

Otis was a dapper individual who always wore the finest of suits and had the most expensive golden cuff links. He never left the house without a tie around his neck, a fresh pair of Stacy Adams, and his golden pinky ring nugget. Otis kept a fresh lineup and had the silkiest wavy hair. His skin was the color and consistency of fine caramel; his cheeks sunk in with deep dimples every time he flashed his perfect pearly white smile. His voice was a smooth, deep baritone that could put any one at ease. His six-foot, four-inch stature and muscular frame was a God-given gift that made him an idol amongst his colleagues.

Otis was a legend in the industry, a man who worked from nothing to come out of nowhere leading the game in money marketing. It was his sharp and witty persona that commanded the room. He was mathematically gifted and considered a genius in his field. Otis was the man, highly respected, feared, and admired. His reputation was flawless in his city, and he was trusted among his peers. Not only was he beautiful to look at, but he was also well-rounded and humble. People found him easy to relate to.

Despite his wealth and status, Otis was always on the scene in his city, helping single mothers and donating turkeys during the holidays, doing his annual toy drive, or mentoring inner city youth. But it was his latest project that really put the city on his back. Otis had recently purchased an old, abandoned government housing sector in the lower east side. He planned to renovate and turn the entire neighborhood into affordable housing for single parents and senior citizens that would include free public transit, an elementary school, a grocery store, a recreational center, an onsite health clinic, and a community garden. You see, Otis was a man for his people, and the people loved Otis McGee! In their eyes, he was a saint!

"Well, Mr. McGee, this is our last session. I hope you are prepared to go deep!" Dr. Blythe exclaimed.

"I am not. But I know it's necessary. I know I need to. So, let's get it done!"

Otis was scared, and the mere thought of him going deeper than what he had already gone in his last sessions made his mouth dry and his armpits sweat. But he knew he had to conquer this. He knew it was long overdue.

"Otis, I know the last time we were here, we left off unpacking your time in foster care with the Reeves family. Would you care to pick up from there?" Dr. Blythe pushed.

"Um."

Otis was sweating. His mouth was dry. Dr. Blythe offered him a drink of water. He obliged. Dr. Blythe instructed him to relax and take a deep breath in, hold it for five seconds, then exhale. He obliged. Dr. Blythe encouraged him to take his time and speak when he was ready.

Ten minutes later, after a serious internal pep talk between Otis and the scared little boy inside, he was ready.

"Well, when I was with them, I was pretty sad and lonely the entire time. I missed my daddy and wanted my mama really bad. I wanted my brothers too, even though they hated me. I just wanted my life back. I knew it was my fault that my life had fallen apart because my daddy loved me more. If I hadn't told on my brothers, I never would have gone there."

Otis paused. Dr. Blythe encouraged him to inhale, hold it for five seconds, and exhale. Otis obliged. Dr. Blythe told him he was doing good and to continue when he was ready.

2 minutes later:

"The dad was nice to me; he tried to make me feel comfortable. The mother was strange. She never liked me. Just always tried to make me be perfect like her boys. 'Sit up straight; don't chew with your mouth open; say yes, ma'am and no, ma'am; say your prayers; pick up your toys; read your scripture; do your homework,' yadda yadda. She just gave me demands all day long. The dad was, like, a weird dude. He was really narcissistic, though at the time, I didn't know that. He loved talking about himself and his accomplishments. Just rubbed it in our faces all day. He would always ask me about my father and what typee of man he was. But he never hurt me either, just always tried to make me like his family."

"Otis, you are doing a great job. How was your relationship with the two boys in the home?" Dr. Blythe encouraged.

Otis paused.

Dr. Blythe reassured him to inhale, hold it, and exhale. Otis obliged. Dr. Blythe reminded Otis to take his time. Otis could feel his heart beating and his head hurting. He wanted to leave, to escape the pain that was bubbling to the surface. But he knew he had to face his demons. He knew he had to speak what he had never been able to speak before and face a hurt he promised himself to forget. After another internal pep talk, a few breathing exercises, and a drink of water, Otis continued.

"Well, they were, um, I don't know. I think they tried to get along with me. They taught me how to pray, and about the Bible and stuff, you know. They, um, they played with me sometimes, but not all the time. They thought I was weird because I didn't go to church and stuff, you know, so I didn't really fit in with them."

"Okay, Otis, that's good. Take your time and continue at your own pace. Tell me about the things you mentioned last session. The things they taught you."

Otis became so nervous that he shot up out of his seat and took a deep breath. He held it and exhaled. He began pacing around the room; his palms were so sweaty, he kept rubbing his hands against his pants. He was aggressively pep-talking himself internally, reminding himself that he could do this. *You can do this, O. You can do this! Your daddy raised a fighter. Fight, O! Fight!* he told himself in his head as he paced around the room.

Dr. Blythe could see that Otis was struggling and was worried he would have a panic attack. He realized he may not be ready to go where he needed to go to heal his past at the present moment.

"Otis, let's just reflect on what we have already discussed. You've done so well today. Perhaps if you are willing, we can have one more session in about a week to fini—"

"No, sir!" Otis yelled, cutting Dr. Blythe off mid-sentence. "I'm sorry, sir, I didn't mean to yell, but I just … I need to do this tonight. Just give me a minute. I can do this."

"Absolutely, Otis; take all the time you need. Remember to breathe. You can pace this entire room as you talk if that helps."

Dr. Blythe began moving things out of Otis's way just in case he needed to let off some steam, or run, or jump, or fall on the floor in tears. He knew an explosion of emotions was coming. What he didn't know was if he was ready to handle the outcome of years of suppressed pain and trauma that were about to pour out of this giant man.

"The brothers, you know, they, um … They showed me special stuff. That's what they called it. They said they learned it from another boy at their church who used to teach them during Bible study. They showed me how to touch them in special places. And, um, they, um … They used to, uh …"

Tears began to fall down Otis's face as he began to relive his abuse in his mind. This was his first cry in a long time about this particular issue. This was his first time feeling these emotions and revisiting this place in decades. He was scared. He needed his daddy. He needed his mama. But all he had was himself, so he continued to pep talk himself and dig deep, encouraging himself to push past the emotions and speak his truth. A truth that he had hidden from everyone he loved, even his own father. A truth he never had the courage to speak. One that only the thought of losing his precious cousin could make him tell another soul.

"They made me touch them, Doc. They made me do things to them with my hands and my mouth that I didn't feel comfortable doing. They said if I didn't do it, I would never go home to my daddy again."

Otis was sobbing at this point as he frantically paced the room, rubbing his hands on his pants. Dr. Blythe wanted to end the session but felt the need to push him further.

"What type of things, Otis?" he pushed.

"Bad things, Doc. Things that I am ashamed of," Otis cried.

"None of those things are your fault, Otis. You were an innocent child," Dr. Blythe encouraged him. "Speaking those things into the atmosphere will get them out. They need to come out so we can process them, so you can be set free."

The thought of freedom enticed Otis. He wanted to be free from this tormented place he had been mentally trapped in since he was a little boy. He wanted to confide in someone. He needed to be understood, for someone to get him and see him for who he really was.

"They told me, 'This is how we show love, Otis.' They said the Bible teacher taught them how to show love; they wanted to teach me too, since I needed to know. They made me touch my privates with their privates and put my mouth on theirs too. Every night before bed, they would tuck me in and touch my private parts with their hands and other objects. One night, their mother came in to put away some laundry, and she caught both of the boys sitting on the side of my bed with their hands down my pants. She screamed and looked directly at me and said, 'Look what you've done to my boys.' She made them leave the room. She told me I was evil and the spawn of Satan. That I was going to burn in hell for teaching her sons such evil things. She spanked me with a wooden paddle until she was tired. I couldn't walk the next two days."

Dr. Blythe could see Otis's demeanor change. His shoulders slumped, and he slowly fell to the floor and sat with his legs crossed. He gazed straight ahead with no direct eye contact. He was speaking softer and slower. His tears were slowly decreasing, and his breathing was slowing down. He was beginning to relax.

"From that day forward, I couldn't see the boys anymore. They moved me to a room in the basement. Mrs. Reeves told me to never tell a soul, and that if I did, I would never go back home. She said I was filthy and needed to repent for my sins before God or face eternal damnation. I never knew if Mr. Reeves found out about what his boys did to me because after that night, I didn't see him or the boys too much, only in passing when I was coming home from school and headed straight to the basement. I couldn't eat dinner with them anymore, or talk to them, or go anywhere at all with them. I was shunned, just a person in their home they did not want."

Otis felt physically weak but spiritually liberated. He fell over in tears and cried the loudest, deepest cry he had ever cried. He cried for what felt like hours. Dr. Blythe did not move, did not speak, did not intervene in his moment. He just let him have it. He was relieved that Otis had finally released this pain and put words to the actions of the Reeves. Clinically, Otis now made perfect sense. He had become a pedophile due to his own experience with childhood sexual abuse that he had suppressed and never processed. He was never therapeutically treated for his trauma. He just kept living as if it never happened, unaware that it had changed his view of life and introduced him to something he did not understand and could not process due to his age and level of psychosocial development. He was a victim who had become a perpetrator of his own abuse.

Once Otis had cried all he could cry, he gathered himself and sat back down in his seat as Dr. Blythe comforted him with tissues and words of affirmation. Dr. Blythe understood that Otis had just released a lot and asked him if he wanted to proceed or schedule one more session to finish processing his trauma. Otis was tired and could not do anymore. Dr. Blythe gave him specific orders.

"Otis, I am going to recommend that you do not work for the next week, that you take a break and find a change of scenery from your normal routine. I would suggest you find a place that is tranquil, where you can relax and reflect on all of the work you have done tonight." Dr. Blythe gave Otis the information for a men's retreat in Biloxi, Mississippi, and recommended Otis go directly there for a week of relaxation and continued therapy.

Dr. Blythe wrapped up their session with clinical information about childhood sexual abuse. He explained to Otis what it was, and the side effects. He also made Otis understand that he was a victim and did not cause his abuse, that his punishment was unwarranted and he did not deserve it. Dr. Blythe informed Otis that what he needed was validation and therapy, that what their mother should have done was comfort him, educate all three of them, and seek help for all of them. He told Otis that maybe Mrs. Reeves spanked him out of fear or anger; maybe she really thought it was Otis fault, but it did not matter what or why because she was wrong and mistaken.

"Otis, I am so proud of the work you have done tonight. But this is only the beginning of your rehabilitation. You need to continue therapy until you get a firm grip on how this abuse has affected you and how it drives your behavior towards your cousin. You need to understand what you have done to her and learn how to move forward in a healthy way because you cannot continue to victimize her or any other child. Do you understand that, Otis?"

Otis was sitting in his chair directly across from Dr. Blythe. With his head down in defeat, he nodded in agreement.

He was a broken man.

He realized in that moment that he had been making Jaines endure the same trauma he had endured as a child. He remembered how he felt in that moment and how hard it had been to deal with his entire life. He felt like he could die right where he sat. He couldn't believe himself. He was disgusted. He was afraid. He knew he couldn't go back home and face Angela or Jaines after being introduced to his new title of "pedophile," so he decided to take Dr. Blythe up on his offer and stay at the retreat for the next week until he figured out his next move!

ELEVEN

"Andre, where are we going?"

Jaines was riding shotgun in the passenger side of Andre's brand-new Benz; he'd just gotten it for his sixteenth birthday. She was scared and worried about what would happen once Otis found out she had run away.

"I don't really know yet. But I have a cousin who lives in Cali. I got a whole lotta money, and both of us are old enough to ride a plane alone."

Andre was barreling down I-95, headed towards anywhere but Jaines's house. Neither one of them felt safe enough to go to the authorities or his parents. Otis had spent most of Jaines's life instilling an irrational fear in her, knowing that if anyone found out what he was doing to her, he would lose it all. He knew he was wrong and there were consequences but couldn't control his urges. And Jaines was so young and impressionable; she believed everything he said and trusted he had a power beyond what he really did. She thought he was untouchable, and given his reputation, she didn't think anyone would believe her. She couldn't bear the feeling of anyone denying her truth.

"Let me call my brother. He and my mom are together somewhere in Chicago. Maybe we can find them."

Jaines was calling her big brother on every number she had for him, but he was constantly getting new phones. She tried her mother, who unfortunately had fallen back to drugs after Jaines's recent suicide attempt. She knew she would be hard to reach. But she kept calling until someone answered.

"Hello? Who is this?"

It was a male's voice.

"Uh, this is Jaines. Um, I'm looking for Lainey."

"Jainey, is that you?"

It was Jeston.

"Yeah, big brother. Is it you?"

"Oh, my God! Jainey! Are you okay? Where are you?" he replied with excitement.

"See, that's the thing, Jeston. I'm not okay. I need you." Jaines was nervous.

Jeston couldn't believe it was his baby sister's sweet voice on the other end of the line. He was flooded with emotion at the sound of her voice and could not hold back tears.

"Put this address in your GPS, Jainey. Text me when you pull up. See you soon, baby sis!"

Jeston gave Jaines the address to his location in Chicago, and she and Andre took off into the unknown. She didn't know where she was going or who would be there; all she knew is her big brother would keep her safe!

Jeston had been in Chicago for the last eight years, chasing down his father since he got out of juvie for running away as a teenager. He was now twenty-three years old and the slickest dope boy on the block. He was a dope boy, but nobody knew it because he was smart and kept a low profile. He only sold low-grade marijuana and any kind of prescription drug he could get his hands on. But he was not the average drug dealer. He had a mind for money and turning over a profit. Every dollar he made he invested in the stock market, trying his luck with different shares. He had done a fair enough amount of research to know the greater the risk, the greater the return, which he learned early on when he took a chance with a major profit he got from his first drop. He was flat broke at the time, living with a long-lost cousin who had taken him in after he arrived in Chicago looking for his father.

It turned out his father was out of prison but hadn't been back home in about five years, and no one knew where he was or what he was doing. His cousin took him in with no question because according to him, "that's what family supposed to do."

He was safe with his cousin who lived in a lower socioeconomic suburban neighborhood in the outskirts of the city. But he was broke and not old enough to secure a real job until his cousin hooked him up with his connect. "You don't work, you don't eat around here. It's every man for himself."

His cousin told him from jump that he could stay there, but he was on his own; he wasn't taking care of a grown man.

Jeston jumped right in the game based off of sheer physical hunger. He was starving. He worked the block and the school hallways, low-key selling what he could, from nickel and dime bags to a few pills here and there. At first, he was only making enough to get a few hot meals and new clothes, but as word got out, he built more and more of a silent reputation. When his connect saw he was turning a quick profit and could be trusted, he offered him five thousand dollars to make a drop. Jeston was scared but needed the money, and he was promised all of it if he did the drop alone.

With the drop done and five thousand dollars cash in his hand, he knew he had to do something with it quick. He couldn't put it in the bank without being scrutinized since he had no ID and no job. He didn't trust his mother to hold it since she was still struggling with her issue. His only option was to find another option. He confided in one of his skateboarding buddies at school that he needed a way to invest some money. His buddy hooked him up with another friend whose father was a stockbroker, and it was uphill from there.

After educating Jeston on the basics of trading and investing, he convinced Jeston to invest all of his money into shares with a fast-growing delivery company that was rapidly taking over the entire region. Jeston knew it was a risk, but he was willing to take it. He had promised himself he would not do anymore drops because it scared him too much and it gave him a bad vibe, but he knew if he invested everything, he would have to start over. It was worth it to him; all he could think about was the earning potential. So, he did it. In the meantime, he continued to work the hallways and the block until he graduated and was old enough to go to the local community college and get a part-time job at the post office sorting mail.

He was making enough to sustain his life for a while. After allowing his initial investment to accrue and grow for almost a decade, he finally had enough money to start a good life for himself as a young, single man on his own. His initial investment had earned him over fifty thousand dollars, which motivated him to continue to invest and trade stocks and bonds. Jeston had become good at weighing risks and profit margins and knew what he was doing. He was well on his way to becoming a millionaire at the age of twenty-three.

He was also saving so much money living with his cousin for so long, who never seemed to have an issue with him being there as long as he pulled his weight. But with his baby sister coming to town soon, he knew he had to get a place that would accommodate her and make her feel comfortable. He didn't know what was going on or what would make her leave her luxurious life with the almighty Cousin Otis, but he could hear in her voice that she was scared. She needed him. Knowing Jaines's past with their mother and all she went through as a kid, he couldn't let his baby sister down. This was just the motivation he needed to get him out of his cousin's house and into a place of his own. He had already abandoned his sister once, and he never forgave himself for leaving her behind. Now, it was time for him to be the man his sister needed him to be. The father neither one of them had ever had.

TWELVE

Angela was boarding her flight back home to Otis and Jaines with a heavy heart. She was so broken over the text log that she had been reading all night long. She couldn't sleep; she had officially been awake for an entire twenty-four hours. She was hoping the plane ride would force her to sleep, but she was worried because she had been calling Jaines and Otis all night and all morning, and neither one of them was answering. She needed to get to Jaines as soon as possible. As soon as she landed, she sped home only to arrive to see squad cars sitting outside of her home. She whipped her McLaren into the driveway and hopped out as quick as she could, terrified that something had happened to Jaines.

"Oh, my God. What happened? Why are you here?" She was frantic.

"Mrs. McGee, calm down. We are here at your request, remember?"

A police officer was standing directly in front of her, calmly placing his hands on her shoulders.

"I called you? I—I'm sorry. I don't remember. I was

panicking last night, and I am a day without sleep. So I—I do—"

"It's okay, ma'am. Is everything okay inside the home?" the officer asked, interrupting her.

"Please come inside with me. I don't know, and I haven't been able to reach my little cousin or husband all night."

After searching the home and finding Jaines's room in disarray and both Jaines and Otis missing, Angela feared the worst. Knowing what she knew now from Jaines's cell records, she knew she needed to find her quick. The police were already on the job, but she also called her friend Peter for backup.

"Police are already looking for her and have put out an APB!" Angela yelled into her phone as she urged Peter to locate Jaines via her last cell phone call.

"Angela, please calm down." Peter had never known Angela to unravel. But he also knew how much she loved Jaines, so he understood. "Her last phone call pinged on a cell tower located northbound I-95."

"I-95 North. Who could she be—Aha! Chicago! She's headed to Chicago!"

Angela also asked Peter to search for Otis's last location and found his last call pinged off of a local cell tower in town around the same time she had spoken with him the night before. He hadn't made a call since then, and his whereabouts remained unknown, proving her suspicions were right and he was driving when they talked. Peter began looking up addresses on Jaines's closest known relatives in Chicago and located her an address registered to a family member of Jeston. Once Angela wrapped up her conversations with the police and her call with Peter, she caught the next flight out to Chicago to find her baby girl.

Meanwhile in Chicago, Jeston had just secured a place for himself and his little sister to stay at for as long as they needed to. It was a nice three-bedroom flat in the uptown business district. It was modern and loaded with upgrades, and close to the local university and shopping, something he thought his sister would like.

Jaines and Andre were still driving to Chicago; they had about two-and-a-half hours left on the trip when she got a text from her brother, giving her the address to the new location. Jaines was so excited to see her brother again after at least five years of no contact since their last visit. He didn't even come to town with her mother when she was hospitalized. She had so many questions. Why did he leave her with Otis? Where were her mother and father? Why had he ignored her for so many years? Didn't he know he was her protector? Jaines was sad, scared, and excited! She couldn't wait to wrap her arms around her superhero big brother who always rescued her in her time of need.

I can't believe the man I have become. I am so ashamed of myself.

Otis was reflecting over his life during his long drive to the men's retreat in Mississippi. He had decided the therapist was right; he needed more time to process his emotions and to dissect whatever mental illness he was dealing with. He wondered if he was sick or evil. He wondered if he should live or if he deserved to die for all he had done to Jaines.

Otis reminisced over his childhood and wondered if he would be this way if he had not gone through all he had been through. Whose fault was it that he was this way? He knew it wasn't his father's because he did all he could possibly do to protect him his entire life, even kidnapping him from child welfare. It wasn't his poor mother's, who had lost her mind and never got it back after her entire family was taken from her in one day. It wasn't his brothers', who were just jealous of him but didn't really know any better. It wasn't God's fault because He never made any mistakes, right? But his life was one huge mistake. If God, the Creator of all things, created him but does not make mistakes, then who or what was the culprit for the outcome of his life?

It was the Reeves family. They did this to him. They turned him into a monster. But it was his fault he ever went there in the first place.

After driving overnight, Otis finally arrived at the retreat and was tired from everything he had just endured. He was not only tired but also just downright angry and ashamed of himself. This entire night was a spiritual awakening for him. But he was torn. Does he tell someone about how he has violated Jaines and lose everything, or does he continue to live this lie, tormenting Jaines for his own benefit? He was beginning to question his life and his worth and if he deserved to be alive. He thought about his last will and testament and realized he needed to make some quick changes.

He had put his phone on airplane mode so he could reflect in peace during his drive. He slowly pulled into a parking space and turned his data back on and was bombarded with alerts. Text after text from Angela, begging him to call her, asking where he was, telling him she was scared and Jaines was missing.

He decided to call her.

"Angela. Hey, baby."

"Otis, where the fuck are you? What have you been doing to Jaines? And don't you dare fucking lie to me!"

"Angela, you don't understand. I—"

Otis couldn't bring himself to confess what he had done. For one, he knew Angela was already working this as a case, and he would lose if he didn't play his cards right. For two, he couldn't bring himself to say what he had been doing.

"Help me understand, O.? What that you're a fucking monster?!" Angela was full-on screaming at the top of her lungs as she walked through the airport. Having just landed in Chicago shewas headed to the address Peter gave her.

"You know Jaines is missing. She ran away. Nobody knows where she is. This is all your fault. I can't believe I married a fucking creep."

"Angela, I don't know what you are talking about. Why are you calling me a creep, baby? What have I done to Jaines? All I've ever done was take care of her." He was playing his cards, but inside, he knew his wife was right. He was a creep. He was worried about Jaines and her whereabouts. He wanted to know where she was, but at this point, he knew he had to keep his distance from her. He knew that from this point forward, it was war. War with his wife. A war that he just might lose.

"You didn't even ask where she is? You don't even care? Ugh! You better get your ducks in a row, because you mark my words: Your days are numbered, motherfucker. Whatever love I had for you was lost when I read Jaines's text messages to Elizaveth about how you have been touching her."

"Angela, I do—" Otis tried to interject, but Angela was livid and ranting.

"Oh, shut up. Nothing you say is the truth. Your whole life is a lie. And I promise I will die proving to the world that you are nothing more than a child molesting, narcissistic sociopath! It's over, O! On my life, you're fucking finished. I better not see you either. If I get to you before the police do, I swear I'm gonna chop your dick off and hand it to you! And you stay away from Jaines. You hear me? Stay away from her!"

Click!

"Fuck!" Otis yelled out loud as he punched the steering wheel of his car until his hand throbbed. He knew what he had to do!

Otis had a ruthless lawyer named Franco Beezy he kept on his payroll in case of a rainy day! And Beezy was not afraid to do whatever it took to win a case. Otis knew that Franco was the best match for Angela. He had never heard his wife this angry; she had never talked to him this way. He knew she no longer saw him as her husband but an enemy. And Angela destroys her enemies! Otis couldn't let her destroy him. He was willing to do whatever it took to maintain his reputation and his millions. He knew he was wrong for hurting Jaines, but he wasn't willing to face the world. He had worked too hard to build his empire. He wasn't about to let it all crumble, even if that's what he truly deserved. He knew how Angela worked, how she got her info illegally through inside connects that she paid under the table, and was willing to use that against her if he had to. And all he needed was probable cause.

Jaines's entire life was probable cause. Her mother was an abusive crackhead, her father a murderer, she bounced from home to home and tried to commit suicide despite the perfect life he had given her. Yeah, she was mentally unstable, and anything she said could not be trusted. The city would believe him; he was their savior. She was nothing more than a troubled teenager. It was her word against his, and his word carried more weight!

Ring ... Ring ...

Otis made a call.

"Franco speaking. Talk to me."

"What up, Beezy? It's O. It's time to go to work!"

THIRTEEN

Angela had finally arrived in Chicago at Jeston's cousin's house only to find out that he moved out a few hours ago because his little sister was coming to stay with him. Angela was pissed she had just missed them but relieved that Jaines was okay and really was on her way to Chicago. Jeston's cousin gave him a call to get his new address and to forewarn him that "some crazy, frantic, fine-ass Black woman is looking for you." Jeston didn't know much about Angela but always felt like she was good people, so he gave his cousin his address.

Angela arrived at the flat before Jaines and Andre. When she arrived, she was surprised to see how handsome Jeston had become. She hadn't really seen him since the last time he and Jaines got together five years ago but could see that he had matured a lot since then. He was tall and light-skinned, with light hazel eyes, short, curly hair, and big, full pink lips. For the first time ever, she realized that he didn't really look like Jaines much at all. They did have a few similar features, like their height and bone structure, but that was it. Who did he look like? She had seen photos of Jaines's dad, and she looked exactly like him. But

Jeston did not look anything like him. But that was the least of her concerns at the moment; she just wanted to find out what he knew and where Jaines was.

"Angela, what are you doing here? Is everything okay with Jaines?" Jeston asked in a smooth, mellow voice as he escorted Angela into his apartment. They both situated themselves at the dining room table, each taking a seat in adjacent chairs facing each other.

"Jeston, there is so much happening. It's really a lot. I don't know where to start, but, um, how was Jaines when you talked to her?"

"She was scared, but I don't think she was hurt or anything. Just said she needed me."

"How is she getting here? Was she on the bus or something? She can't drive," Angela asked with tears in her eyes.

"Oh, I don't know. I didn't know she wasn't driving yet. Let me call her." Jeston was reaching for his phone, but Angela stopped him.

"No, don't call her; she will get suspicious. I don't want her to know I'm here. She may be scared to come if she knows I am here." Angela was worried about Jaines's fragile mental state. She didn't know if Jaines thought she may have known about what Otis was doing to her.

Jeston and Angela talked and got all caught up on his life and what he had been doing the past few years. Angela learned he was a smart and savvy trader who sold low-grade drugs on the low, but he was done with dealing since his sister was coming to live with him. He was ready to be a man for her and take care of her the right way. Jeston told Angela that his mother had also moved back to Chicago with her family after Jaines's suicide attempt because she went a little mental. The stress of it all made her relapse, and she was now somewhere on the streets of Chicago, smoking crack again. Jeston was sad about it, but also resented her for all of the things she used to do to Jaines and how she abandoned them. He had learned to not care about what his mother was doing.

Jeston told Angela how he tried to locate his father but couldn't, which is how he ended up with a cousin he hardly knew, but was grateful because he was a good dude who gave him a place to stay. He told her that for the moment, he was going to focus on taking care of Jaines but would soon resume his search for their father. Angela was so impressed with Jeston and how well-rounded he was, given the life he was handed. She couldn't help but to feel sorry for him for all that he had been through, but she was also proud of the man he had become all on his own.

"Wait. Just got a text. Jaines is pulling up."

Jeston headed downstairs to greet his baby sister while Angela waited inside. As Jeston approached Jaines and Andre sitting in the car, he was blown away by how beautiful his little sister was. He was so struck by her that he didn't even notice Andre sitting in the driver's seat. Jeston ran to Jaines's side of the car and opened the door as quickly as he could, hardly giving her enough time to unbuckle her seatbelt and get out. As soon as she was loose, he snatched her up lovingly into his arms and spun her around like he used to do when they were little.

"Jainey, my Jainey," is all he could say before tears fell down his face as they stood there, hugging each other tightly.

They both cried, releasing tears of joy and sadness. The joy of being together again and the sadness of not seeing each other for so long. Andre sat and watched their embrace as he finally called his mother to tell her where he was.

"Mom."

"Andre, where are you, son? I'm worried sick."

"I'm fine, Mom. I'm in Chicago!"

"Boy, what the hell are you doing in Chicago? Wait until your father finds out about this. You can kiss that car goodbye."

"Ma, listen to me. I'm sorry. But please trust me, I had to do this. I'll explain later."

"Son! Hear me and hear me well. You do exactly what I am about to tell you. You hear me?" His mother was livid.

"Yes, ma'am." Andre was petrified.

"Go directly to the Chicago airport, and wait for me there. I am flying in to meet you. We will drive back home together, which will give you plenty of time to explain why you had to do this!"

"Yes, ma'am," Andre replied with his voice shaking and his heart racing. He took a hard swallow. He knew he was in deep trouble.

He had never disobeyed his parents before or even gotten a spanking. He learned early on that good behavior reaped good rewards. He made obedience a habit. He never talked back, never challenged the status quo, and always got everything he wanted. His parents always told him it was "because you're such a good kid." He was so accustomed to doing the right thing that the thought of breaking a rule scared him. This was the most daring thing he had ever done. He was in love with Jaines, and he was willing to risk it all to save her from the hell she lived in. He had heard before that love would make you do crazy things, so it must be that he loved her, because driving to Chicago without telling his parents was the craziest thing he had ever done. He was nervous about what the consequences would be, and as much as he wanted to stay in Chicago with Jaines, he knew it would be better for him to just do what his mother said.

"Jaines, I gotta go. I'm sorry. I can't stay," Andre said as he got out of the car and grabbed Jaines's bag from the back seat. The sound of his voice shook Jaines and Jeston out of their trance and made them release their embrace.

"Jeston, this is Andre, my friend from school. Andre, this is my big brother, Jeston," Jaines introduced her brother and Andre as they shook hands and stared each other in the eyes.

"Hey, man. Thanks for taking care of my little sister. What do I owe you for the trip?" Jeston was squeezing Andre's hand firmly, asserting his authority.

"Nah, man. You don't me nothing," Andre replied as he looked over at Jaines. "I'll do anything for Jaines." Andre released his hand from Jeston's grip, hugged Jaines, and kissed her on her forehead.

"I gotta go, Jaines." He slowly walked to his car, never taking his eyes off Jaines until he drove out of sight.

"Ah, shit, little sis. This guy is in love with you. You do know that, right?" Jeston was shaking his head and laughing in disbelief that his little sister had some dude's nose wide open. Jaines hid her face in her hands in embarrassment.

Jeston and Jaines locked arms as he led her upstairs to their new place. Jaines didn't know what it meant to be loved. The only love she had ever really known from a man was the love Otis gave her. And she had had enough of that.

"Oh, my God! Jaines! Are you okay, baby?!"

Angela ran to Jaines and wrapped her up in a tight embrace as she looked her over to see if she was okay. Jaines was shocked to see Angela there and felt ambushed by her brother. *Why didn't he tell me? Why is she here? How did she know where to find me? Did Otis send her?* Jaines's head was racing with questions.

"Angela, I'm fine. I just needed to see Jeston."

"Listen, Jaines, it's okay. You can talk to me. I know about you and O. I mean, I just found out."

Jaines was shook and paralyzed with fear. She was frozen in place, just standing there, staring at Angela with tears rolling down her face. She couldn't talk. She felt like she was about to go back to that safe place in her mind she went to after her grandmother passed. Angela knew this look all too well, and if she didn't act fast, she was going to lose Jaines to a permanent silence. She had to find the words to say to make Jaines feel safe. She grabbed Jaines by the shoulders and shook her softly.

"Stay with me, Jaines. Listen to me, baby girl. Otis is not here. You're safe now. He can't hurt you anymore!"

With those words, Jaines slowly came back to reality, and her fear began to subside. She knew she could trust Angela. She had never crossed her and always had her back. She also knew that there was no way Angela could have known before now about Otis because he was such a master manipulator.

Jeston was standing back, confused about what was going

on. "Wait, what do you mean, 'he can't hurt her'? Jaines, what did he do to you?" Jeston had moved Angela out of the way and was now standing in front of Jaines, gripping her shoulders, staring her in the eyes. "What did he do to you, sis?" he asked her softly, now wiping her tears from her face and pushing her head to his shoulder.

"lets all just calm down. Here come let's sit and talk so we can all figure this out." Angela suggested as the trio moved to the living room and sat right next to each other on the sofa. Angela could feel the level of heightened emotions in the room as they all just sat in silence until Jeston broke it.

"somebody please tell me what's going on?"

"Jaines, baby its okay. I know what O is doing to you. I found out. Because I got a copy of your cell phone records. I saw the texts between you and Elizaveth." Angela tried to encourage Jaines that she was safe to speak. But that revelation just made Jaines cry harder. She was having a full-on emotional breakdown. Crying tears that she had kept silent since she was a little girl. Crying tears for every time her mother hit her for no reason or talked ugly to her. Tears for every time Otis violated her body. Tears of relief that someone else finally knew and believed her. Tears of freedom because maybe her nightmare life was finally over. Tears for her mother who abandoned her, and her father who she never knew. Tears for her grandmother who died, and she couldn't help. She cried a deep soul cry. Her cries soon turned to screams of anger and rage as she remembered all that she had been through.

"It's okay baby. Let it out." Angela knew that this was an

emotional breakthrough that Jaines needed and had been afraid to let herself have for years. Jeston just watched in disbelief as his little sister lost all self-control. Jaines, now up and moving around the apartment screaming, and stomping, and punching the walls, was yelling at the top of her lungs that she hated Otis. She switched from screaming, to crying, to laughing hysterically, back to crying again. Jeston was so scared he grabbed her and held her so she wouldn't hurt herself.

"should we call 911 Angela?"

"No Jeston, just let her have her moment. She needs to let this out."

Jeston and Angela began moving everything out of Jaines way that could possibly cause her injury; then locked hands and formed a circle around her, and carefully moved around the room with her until she was tired and fell to the floor sobbing. It was heartbreaking for Jeston and Angela to see her in so much pain. After she had calmed down, she was too exhausted to talk. Angela and Jeston lead her to the bedroom so she could rest for the evening. After laying Jaines down Angela decided to tell Jeston what she knew. She explained to him that she had no inclination that anything was happening with Jaines until she attempted suicide. That was her first red flag that something was wrong. But until then she was just a typical teenager other than being awkwardly shy and quiet, she showed no signs of being sexually abused. She told him how at the hospital Otis was acting strange and how their mother said something that struck her as odd. Something about Otis touching on Jaines like he used to touch her. However, Otis denied that he ever did. But she couldn't let it die and started digging on her own to find out what could have caused Jaines to want to end her life. She also told him about her friend Elizaveth and how her mother had forbidden her to come over to the house for some reason. All the signs were pointing to Otis being the culprit; but she had no proof until she got Jaines cell phone records. That's when she saw the messages, she was sending to her best friend. That was the proof she needed to satisfy her suspicions of her husband's guilt.

Jeston was in shock that Otis was capable of doing these things. And could not believe what he was hearing or that he even idolized someone like him. But he was only in shock for a moment before it turned to anger!

"Jeston where are you going?" Angela was following Jeston to the door after he shot up off of the couch to grab his keys

"I'm going to find Otis. He violated my baby sister. He gotta die!"

Angela tried to stop Jeston but he was too strong; he pushed right passed her and ran out of the door. She knew she needed to call the police at this point before somebody got hurt.

Jeston was furious as he sped down the streets of his neighborhood heading to the Southside of Chicago to see his homie "Big Rod" who was always posted up at the trap house. He gave him a call since he knew he would have what he needed.

"Yo Rod I'm on my way. I need that heat bro."

"I got you homie, text me when you pull up." Rod knew what was up and he had just what Jeston needed.

Angela was pacing back in forth in the living room of Jestons apartment waiting for the police to arrive. She tried calling Otis out of sheer anger to give him a piece of her mind, but it was going straight to voice mail. And she knew better than to leave him an angry message if she was going to be the one to represent Jaines in court; which she fully planned to do. She had to be smart about this and not allow her emotions to control her. She knew this would be the hardest case she has ever tried. Her husband, the man she has loved for years; against her cousin who she loved like her very own daughter. How could he do this? Why would he? She wondered as she waited. But that didn't matter anymore, all that mattered now that he paid for what he has done to Jaines, she deserved justice. She had never lost a case before; but Angela knew that if she was going to win this one, she would need all the help she could get; that she would have to do everything with precision to take her husband down. It was war. Husband against wife; and she was determined to get justice for Jaines at all costs. When the police finally arrived to Jestons apartment, she told them everything. They woke Jaines up and they all went down to the police station to take a statement. Angela also had Jaines take a lie detector test, and a physical examination. Angela was adamant that Otis was an immediate threat to society and a flight risk due to his money and power. She would not leave until charges were filed and warrant for his arrest was issued. Once she had the paper work and proof of charges filed in her hand; it was on!

"Hey Stacy its Angela; you still work for Chanel 26 News in Chicago?"

"Hey girl, yeah I'm still here. Why what's up. What you got?"

"I got the inside scoop on one hell of a story. How soon can you run it."

"Depending on the validity of it, I can run it tonight in our evening segment."

"Good, trust me its valid."

"Okay, how soon can you meet me on set?"

"Give me about an hour and I'll be there."

"Nice. See you in an hour!"

Stacy knew she could trust Angela. Her reputation spoke for her. Not only was she married to the most powerful black man in Nathanville North Carolina; but she was also known to deliver the truth and always able back up any claim with factual evidence. Stacy knew that if it was coming from Angela, it was going to be good. This could be the opportunity of a lifetime! She didn't care how juicy it was, who it was going to affect. All that mattered was that she was breaking it tonight at 9, and she couldn't wait to be the first to spill the tea!

FOURTEEN

Otis had just met up with his lawyer Franco, for a quick consultation before he snuck away to board a plane to Mexico for a few weeks. He could feel in his spirit that he needed to get out of sight and lay low for a little while until things settled down.

"Listen Franco; there are some allegations being made about me by my cousin." Otis was explaining to Franco, who was sitting directly across from him at his desk in his corner office with his luxurious view of downtown North Carolina.

"Well, it must be pretty serious if you drove all night to get here brother." Franco was curious to know what had Otis in such a frazzled state. He had never known Otis to be shaken by anything. But he could clearly see that he was physically tired, and emotionally a little off. Franco was the kind of man who would do whatever the money paid him to do. He had learned years ago to remove all emotions from his line of work. He never got attached to anyone or anything; for him it was always business, and business was always a pleasure when the money was right. And Otis paid well; he never bounced a check. Of all of Franco's clients, he was the most loyal to Otis because he paid him year-round even when he did not have a case he needed him to fight.

"it's serious, could ruin me if it catches wind." Otis was exhausted from driving back to North Carolina from the retreat all night, and from the emotional work he had done in therapy. He knew he had to get out of the sight before Angela dropped a dime to the authorities on him. He wasn't worried about being arrested because he had plenty of bail money. But he was worried about his reputation. This is the type of stain on a reputation that one can never remove. He knew it would ruin him and follow him for the rest of his life.

"Well, what's the allegation, and how true is it?"

"First of all. It's not true at all, and it's Jaines word against mine. She is telling people that I was touching her inappriately. She has my wife believing her. And I have a feeling that they are going to go to the police soon." Otis was staring Franco directly in his eyes to see how he would react to what he said. And just as he expected, he didn't flinch and showed no emotion.

"Well, this is definitely the type of thing that can ruin a man like you! Especially if I wasn't your lawyer. But you're in luck brother! Because I am your lawyer." Franco was making light of the situation with a sly laugh, as he leaned back in his chair. However, Otis did not repay the same sentiment. He was really scared; and needed Franco to take this seriously.

"Franco, man you don't understand. My wife is on my little cousins' side. She will probably represent her in court, and if I know her like I think I do, she has already filed charges against me and it's only a matter of time before I'm being fingerprinted. And I cannot have my mugshot all over the nightly news!"

"tell me Otis, what's more important to you at the present moment. Your freedom; or your wife?"

"My reputation; everything I've worked for is built upon that."

"Okay then, you leave your wife, your freedom, and your reputation to me. If she decides to prosecute you in court. She will have to go through me. And unlike everybody else I am not scared of Angela Mcgee!" Franco was suddenly very serious and sinister in his response. Which made Otis a bit nervous for Angela because he knew how Franco operated.

"Look Franco, nobody has to get hurt. I just want justice. This thing they are saying is not true. I just," Otis paused and signed a deep sigh of distress. "Look if this gets to the point of a trial I just want to walk." Otis was looking at Franco with pleading eyes. Pleading for him to take it easy on his wife. After all he still loved Angela and the truth is he really was guilty, and Angela was totally right for helping Jaines. He just couldn't fathom losing his life's work to one little mistake.

"Trust me O. It won't even get that far. This will be over before it even starts." Franco and Otis discussed the terms of his potential case for another hour. Before they wrapped up around 8:30 PM, leaving Otis worried about his impending doom as he headed to his private landing strip to board a his jet out of North Carolina..

Meanwhile in Chicago, Angela had just given Stacy the inside scoop to the hottest story of the year. And in 30 minutes; Stacy was about to drop a bomb on a hometown hero. Angela and Jaines were headed back to Jestons place for the night to reflect and prepare for what was to come..

"Jaines, baby please talk to me. Tell me how you are feeling about all of this?" Jaines didn't speak, she just stared out of the window and shrugged her shoulders. She wasn't quite in thatsafe place in her mind, but she felt like one more catastrophic event would send her there for eternity. In her heart she was relieved because she knew Angela and Jeston would take care of her; and protect her from Otis. At least one part of her nightmare was over. But she was also scared because she knew that so many parts to this nightmare were only just beginning.

"I'm just scared Angela. I don't know what to expect." Jaines said, still gazing.

"You listen to me Jaines. You don't have to worry about anything. Just lay low and focus on your mental health. You need to heal. You will have to be strong enough to face Otis in court. He will deny any allegation of abuse from you. He will probably slander you too. He will do whatever it takes to maintain the position of power he has acquired in his lifetime. Trust me; you think you have seen the worst of him; but you haven't Jaines."

"what if no one believes me Angela? What if they think I made it all up?"

"Who cares what they think. We know the truth, and the truth always prevails. No matter what happens in the coming weeks months, hell even years. You just trust God to avenge you little girl. You did nothing to deserve this, and God will work it all in your favor. Besides, I am your lawyer, and I will stop at nothing to take your scumbag cousin down." Angela was gripping her steering wheel with all of her might; her anger was causing her to drive faster without her realizing. Jaines could see fire in Angela's eyes. . She was afraid of what the days ahead. How could she possibly prepare herself to face Otis in court? How could she deal with the pain of people not believing her? Would they win? Would he be found guilty? Jaines heart was full of emotion and wonder as Angela sped down the highway back to her bothers house. 20 minutes of silence later, Angela's voice broke into atmosphere and interrupted Jaines's racing thoughts.

"Jaines you gotta be tough okay. This is about to be so hard. Harder than you can imagine. But you can do this. I believe in you. This will teach you how to use your voice! This will show you the woman God created you to be! And he created you to be strong and fearless! You hear me? So, whatever it takes, you just be ready to do your part to take that motherfucker down!"

Jeston, still fuming with rage had just pulled up to Big Rods spot to get what he needed to take care of Otis. He knew that Big Rods spot was the least safe on the entire block and would never go there in broad daylight or under any other circumstances but in this case, there were no limitations because Otis had to pay. As he was approaching the trap house, he could smell the strong aroma of marijuana, he could hear trap music blasting from the inside as dope heads entered in and out of the front door in a hurry. Rushing in to get their product of choice, and rushing out to go smoke it, or shoot it up, or however they got high. Jeston entered the living room, which was dimly lit with a one dingy old beat-up sofa being used as a bed by some nameless addict who probably used too much supply.

As he continued down the hall he passed the kitchen which

was filthy and smelled like old trash and vomit. Big Rod was always posted up in the back room near the back door so he could easily escape if he needed to. That was also the safest room to hide the heavy artillery, and his vast array of illegal drugs. But before he could enter the room, he had to establish himself as someone who Rod had worked with before.

"What's the word?" He was asked by one of Rod's workers who was guarding the door with a semi-automatic rifle.

"Red rum." Jeston only knew it because Big Rod had just texted it to him on the way over. Big Rod was clever enough to know that an addict will talk to anyone, even the Feds, so he changed his code word daily and would only sell product to the ones who knew it. Jeston was always curious as to how people found out the new word, but right now wasn't the time to ask.

"Okay. You good, homie." The guard let him past the door to Rod.

"Yo! What up, J!" Big Rod was exactly like his name said. Big. Legally named Rodrick Finnagan, he was a six-foot-four, three-hundred-and-fifty-pound Black man with a hint of German from his mother's side. You could only see the German in his hair, which was a silky-smooth, deep, wavy texture, but his skin was a dark as night. Big Rod had been in the game for decades and had only been caught up once. He was a kind fellow who sold drugs to support his family. He wasn't ruthless and let a lot of addicts off the hook for debts they owed him. He was as good as a dope dealer could be.

"What up, big homie? What you got for me?" Jeston was focused on getting an unregistered firearm so he could finish his cousin. Big Rod was wiping down the weapon and giving Jeston the details, while simultaneously serving clients. Addicts were moving in and out of the back room swiftly to get their product as discreetly as possible. All kinds of addicts: lawyer addicts, doctor addicts, stripper addicts, college student addicts. One thing Jeston learned about a drug habit as a dealer is that it doesn't discriminate. It is limitless; it breaks all boundaries and pushes past any barrier.

"Aye, yo, Rod, this chick trying get past me. She don't know the word, bro." The guard was lightly tussling with a woman trying to get into the back room to get some work, but she didn't know the code word. However, she was desperate to get her fix, even willing to take on the doorman and his war weapon.

"Hold up, J. Let me see what's up." Big Rod calmly put the weapon down to investigate the issue at the door. When he got to the door, he immediately recognized the client fighting with the guard.

"Aw, shit. She good, man. Let her in."

The guard loosened his grip on her tiny, emaciated arm at Rod's command and let her in. Rod went right back to cleaning the weapon for Jeston while simultaneously preparing a bag of dope for his client, who was talking trash about the doorman.

"Rod, who the hell is this idiot you got working the door? He almost got messed up!" The client was staggering into the room, rubbing her arm in frustration that the doorman had the audacity to not know who she was.

Jeston was focused on securing his weapon and honestly was annoyed by all of the distractions. He hated being at Big Rod's for too long because he knew it wasn't a safe place. He was so focused that he had blocked out all the distractions in the room and had his eyes fixated on Rod's hands cleaning and loading his gun; he didn't even hear the client making a fuss in the background.

"Aw, shit. You hell, Lainey." Big Rod was laughing and encouraging the client as she stepped closer to where he and Jeston were doing business. Jeston was zoned out, but thought he heard something familiar. He thought he heard Big Rod say "Lainey." The sound of that name shook Jeston out of his trance, and he swiftly turned around to see who this client was.

"Mama!"

Jeston was in complete shock to see his mother standing right behind him, cracked out. His heart immediately broke, and tears fell down his face. He hadn't seen her in so long, and she was merely unrecognizable. She stood there in shock too, almost like she didn't know who he was. She was so thin, her hair disheveled and matted on top of her head. She was dizzily standing in dingy oversized sweatpants and a filthy old T-shirt full of holes and nasty stains. She had a shoe on one foot and only a sock on the other. Her face was sunken in, and her eyes were bulging. All her beauty had been lost to the streets. To crack. To hopelessness.

"Mama, what the fuck are you doing here?"

Jeston's sadness quickly turned into confusion as he looked back at Rod, who was just as in shock as they were. He was frozen, looking back and forth at the two of them, searching for any kind of resemblance.

"Yo, J, I meant no disrespect, bro. I had no idea this was your mama." Big Rod was pleading his case to his homeboy. He and Jeston had been good friends for a few years, and Rod was loyal to his core; he wanted Jeston to know he would never intentionally sell crack to his mother.

Lainey was still puzzled as to what was happening. She was coming down off her last high and just wanted to get high again. She was visibly puzzled but tried to be present in the moment.

"Jeston, son, is that you?" she said, still rubbing her arm and squinting her eyes as if that would make him appear more familiar to her.

"Yo, Lainey, um … Y'all gotta raise up outta here. I can't serve you no more." Big Rod had grown frustrated because he noticed he was losing clients due to the hold up, prompting him to urge Jeston and his mother to continue their saga elsewhere.

"But hold up, J. Don't forget this. Don't sweat it, homie; it's on me. I owe you one." Big Rod had handed J the unregistered and fully loaded nine-millimeter pistol before he left. He decided to waive all fees since he'd been unknowingly aiding Jeston's mother in her own demise, which he felt really bad for, since Big Rod was the type of dealer who had a heart.

"I'm so sorry, homie. I really am. Get at me later, bro. And let me know if you need any more help with that issue," Big Rod expressed to Jeston as they dapped each other up with no hard feelings.

Jeston grabbed his mother by the arm and pulled her out of the trap house. Both Jeston and his mother were silent as he dragged her out of the back room and down the hall towards the front door. She was mad that she couldn't get any drugs but knew this was a fight she would lose. Strategically, she decided to go along with Jeston for the moment until she could make her escape.

Just as they were about to head out the door, Jeston stopped.

"Here. Put this on." He gave his mother his shoes and his coat. He knelt down to tie his shoes for her, then stood to affix his coat on her properly. It was fall in Chicago; there was a slight evening wind chill, and the weather was below sixty degrees. He couldn't have his mother walking around with no shoes and coat. As he led her out of the door and to the car, he couldn't help but wonder what he was going to do with her. He knew she was beyond his scope of fixing. She needed professional help. With nowhere else to turn, he gave Angela a call.

"Angela, I ran into my mother. I have her with me now, but she's a mess. I don't even think she knows who I am. I don't know what to do."

Jeston had driven a few miles down the road to a local gas station to get away from the trap house. He was sitting in the car with his mother, whom he had strapped in, and locked the doors and windows, knowing fully that the only thing her mind was getting high and that she was a flight risk.

Angela and Jaines were back at his place and were preparing for bed. Angela quietly stepped outside on the balcany to take the call, being careful not to add to Jaines' despair.

"Man, J. How the heck did you run into her?"

"Long story, Angela. Just tell me what to do."

"Hell, I don't know. I've never dealt with a crackhead before. Sorry; that was rude."

"It's fine."

"What's her mental state like? Do you think it's safe to bring her here?"

"Um, she's quiet right now, probably still high or something. I'm sure she's trying to plan an escape, but I don't want to lose her again. Jaines can't see her like this. I can't bring her there."

"Um … Okay. Just let me think."

They both paused for a few minutes as Angela ran down a list of Chicago resources in her mind.

"Okay, Jeston, stay where you are. Let me call a friend in the city that owes me a favor. I'll call you right back."

As Jeston hung up the phone and decided to try to break into his mother's space with conversation.

"Mama, do you know who I am?" he asked his mother, who was in a daze, staring out of the window and still rubbing her arm.

"Yeah, son, I know you. How could I forget my only son?" Lainey was slowly coming back to reality but didn't remember how she and Jeston ended up together. "Where did you find me at, son?" she asked with genuine concern.

"It doesn't matter, Mama. Do you want to come with me to my house?" Jeston asked her, knowing full well he was not about to take his mother to his house.

"No, son, I need to go home. I got somebody waiting on me there. Just let me out here. I can walk."

Lainey needed a fix. She hadn't lived in reality in quite some time. She had been spending her days numbing all of her emotional and mental anguish with any kind of drug she could get her hands on, primarily crack, since it was cheap. Her only issue was that the high was so quick, she had to keep getting high to stay high.

"Hell no. I'm not letting you out here. You shouldn't even

be walking these streets this late, Mama." Jeston was so saddened at his mother's current state. And if Angela didn't call him back soon, he was going to take matters into his own hands.

"Mama, just go to sleep or something. I'm gonna take you somewhere to get to some food." He lied to keep her calm. After waiting in awkward silence for another ten minutes or so, his phone finally rang.

"Jeston, take her to the address I'm about to text you. It's a rehabilitation center on the west side of town. It's the best I could do on such short notice. Since the ownerowner owes me a big one, Lainey is good to check in for free. Usually, they have to agree to go, but he is going to bend the rules for us.. Don't tell her where you are taking her. Just get her there and drop her off; they will do the rest. Text me when you are pulling up, and I will make sure they are waiting outside when you arrive."

With the address plugged into his GPS and his mother fading away into an abyss of sleep, Jeston was off to the rehab center. He was scared about how she would respond when she got here, but he knew it was the only chance he had to save her life. Making Otis pay for what he did to Jaines would have to wait. But as soon as he dropped his mother off, he would be back on the hunt for his cousin's head.

FIFTEEN

"Good evening, Chicago. I am Stacy Whittaker, and you're watching Channel 26 News Now. Thank you for joining me this evening for the latest hot topics in local and celebrity news. Stay tuned for the exclusive on recent developments in the shocking allegations being made about a local hometown hero. You don't want to miss this."

Stacy was excited to be the first with an exclusive story on someone like Otis McGee, who had made a name for himself after overcoming the harsh poverty of the Chicago streets to become a brilliant and successful international business mogul. He was known and respected by everyone — the locals, politicians, and celebrities alike. Due to his status, Stacy would not agree to dropping the story first without solid evidence that it was true; she didn't want the backlash of delivering fake news on a pseudo-celebrity. After reading the affidavit and seeing that charges had been filed in Chicago and an APB was put out earlier in North Carolina, she felt safe enough to run with it. She and Angela also cleared with the Chicago Police Department to be the first to make the public aware of the warrant for Otis's arrest, and had the police chief on standby to make a public statement about the charges being filed.

"Earlier this week, Channel 26 was given the exclusive on recent allegations of sexual misconduct of none other than Chicago's own Otis McGee. You may know McGee from his rise to fame as a businessman and money mogul in North Carolina. He has been admired for his perseverance, charisma, and financial prowess. But could it be, that our favorite money mogul is a monster in disguise? In an affidavit obtained by our reporters, it has been alleged that Otis McGee has been engaging in ongoing sexual abuse with a underaged victim, who will remain unidentified. The victim alleges that McGee has been abusing her consistently over the last ten years of her life. The report not only alleges sexual abuse but also child endangerment, harassment, blackmail, and false imprisonment. Our local Chief of Police, Dan Russel, has more. Over to you, Dan."

The local police chief was tasked with unwanted role of public speaker. He stood solemnly in front of the local police department with no enthusiam. Reluctantly accepting this transfer of correspondence; knowing this was a pandora's box of public relations nightmares his precinct was unprepared to manage.

"It is true, Stacy, that Otis McGee has been officially charged with several counts of sexual abuse of a minor, indecency with a child, one count of child endangerment, black mail, and one count of false imprisonment. The Chicago Police Department has issued a warrant for his arrest. If anyone knows the whereabouts of the suspect, please contact the police department immediately. Thank you. That's all we have at this time."

"Well, there you have it, folks. You heard it here first. I am Stacy Whittaker with Channel 26 News Now. Stay tuned for more breaking stories after this quick commercial break."

Angela and Jaines were sitting side by side on the sofa, hugging each other around the waist and gripping each other tightly when the news broke. They couldn't believe that it was actually happening. The public was finally being made aware of the kind of monster Otis really was. Jaines was scared and relieved all at once. Angela was nervous because she knew it was game time, and she had just made one hell of a first move. She knew Otis was going to come for her jugular with all he had, but she was ready. With Jeston being tied up with his mother and hunting down Otis, and her needing to prepare for the case, Angela had to find a safe place for Jaines. She couldn't be here in Chicago alone. She needed to be under the care of a therapist and someone with a watchful eye. It was time for her to make a call that she had avoided for over a decade. She was desperate but knew what needed to be done.

Ring ... ring ... ring ...

"Hello?" an older male voice answered the line.

"Hello, Dad? It's me, Angela."

"Angela, baby, is that you?" her dad asked, in shock to hear her voice for the first time in over a decade.

After speaking briefly with her father and explaining to him the recent unfolding of events, he agreed to allow Jaines to stay with them until the dust settled and it was safe for her to return. Angela had made plans to fly back home within the next few days to drop Jaines off before she headed back to North Carolina to build a case against her husband.

Leeland was still shaken by hearing his baby girl's voice after what felt like an eternity of her shutting him and her mother out of their lives. He and his wife had been retired for a few years and were living the good life of not being fiscally responsible for anyone but themselves. They were not looking forward to taking on an emotionally disturbed teenager but were willing to do anything to get back into Angela's good graces. After all, they figured they owed Angela after what they put her through.

Angela was not excited about seeing her parents again, after years of isolating them our of her life.She was terrified of the emotions she would have to process. But she couldn't let it phase her. She owed it to Jaines to do what was best for her and seek vengeance on her behalf. Angela was secretly dealing with the guilt of not knowing Otis was abusing Jaines. She was disgusted with herself for loving and making love to a monster. How could she not see who he really was? How could she not see that Jaines was being abused? Was she that consumed with work that she had become oblivious to what was really happening in her own home? She was ashamed of herself and her husband. She knew she would also be guilty by association and was preparing to deal with the backlash. But right now, all that mattered was getting Jaines somewhere safe. And she knew that her parents, as much as she still despised them, were her only option.

Back in North Carolina, the city of Nathanville was shaken by the news of Otis's recent allegations. The streets were talking and the story was spreading like wildfire. Local patrons were trying to figure out who this underaged teen could possibly be. How come they didn't mention Otis's wife, and where was his little cousin? Not even twenty-four hours after the story broke, people were already filling in the blanks with their own renditions of what was really going on. The story had already gone viral on social media and was being retweeted at a groundbreaking rate. It was the talk of the town in Nathanville and the city of Chicago — and soon, the entire world.

Otis's private jet had just landed in Mexico when he got a call from Franco.

"Yo, O. Your wife is playing chess, not checkers, brother. You might want to sit down for this one." Franco was sitting at his desk, watching Stacy drop the Otis bomb on YouTube for the fifteenth time.

"I just landed, my phone is blowing up, man." Otis expressed with annoyance as gathered his bags from the plane.

"Look, O, the local news in Chi-Town got wind of the allegations — and even worse, 5-0 already put a warrant out for your arrest." Franco was blindsided by this, but he liked a challenge and was already working out how to rise to the occasion.

"Damn, a warrant? On what evidence? Don't you need valid evidence for a warrant?" Otis was rattled. Even though he knew Angela was on his tail, he hadn't expected things to be unfolding so expeditiously.

"Honestly, O, I don't know what the evidence is. But don't worry about that. That's my problem. You just get somewhere and lay low for a few hours. But don't get too comfortable. I am going to find a way to spin this in your favor. You being in Mexico may just work for you."

"Help me understand how, Franco."

"Well, it's like this: There is a warrant for you in the States, but you're on vacation out of the country. If you leave vacation early to turn yourself in, then it will look like you have nothing to hide."

"Okay. So, what's the play?"

"I am about to contact the police department right now and let them know you will be returning to the States this as soon as possible to turn yourself in. I will also ask to make a public statement on your behalf in an attempt to begin clearing your name."

"Shit, man. I gotta go to jail, Franco? You know that's not my thing." Otis was hoping there was another option.

"Unfortunately, brother, you will have to be booked. But don't worry; you will be released right away once we pay the bail, which I already have prepared. By the way, it's a possible two hundred and fifty thousand."

"Holy shit, man. Look, Franco, I am not built for this. You do what I pay you to do. I don't want to be in that damn jail any longer than twenty-four hours. You hear me?"

"Trust me, O, it's the best thing to do. Give me a few hours, and I'll be in touch. And you will be processed in and out. I will see to that myself!"

Otis owned a bungalow in the countryside of Mexico that he liked to travel to when he needed to escape reality. He figured he would lie low there for a few hours and wait for Franco to give him his next move. Meanwhile, Franco placed a call to the police department with his demands on behalf of his client. Telling them to expect Otis to turn himself in within a few days; however, he demanded they not release any information to the public on behalf of his client and that he be given the opportunity to speak on his behalf at a press conference in front of the police station once Otis turned himself in. The police chief agreed to those terms, of course, because he was a friend of Otis's and knew he was a good man. All of this must've just been some huge misunderstanding.

Franco made a call to Otis.

"Listen O, you have a little time to rest, then you need to fly back and meet me at the back of the Chicago Police Department within the next forty-eight hours."."

Otis was scared reluctant he trusted that Franco would ensure he wouldn't be locked down for long. Otis wanted to enjoy his last moments of freedom, but he couldn't rest without talking to his therapist first. He needed help processing what he had revealed to him and all of the recent events.

Otis video-called Dr. Blythe.

"Oh, hi, Otis. Wow. You don't look so good." Dr. Blythe was pretending that he hadn't heard the news.

"Doc, I'm falling apart. It's all falling apart. Help me. Please." Otis was sitting on the patio of his bungalow, looking out among beautiful hills wondering how his life had come to this. He felt as if he was on the verge of a mental breakdown and wanted the doctor to tell him what to do.

"Otis, tell me what is happening in your mind right now." Dr. Blythe was logging notes in his journal from a few other sessions and had about thirty minutes before his next session began. He had already seen the news and heard the allegations, and knew Otis was a wanted man.

Otis was confident that Dr. Blythe would not report his abuse to the authorities because he paid him a hefty fee not to do so. However, unbeknownst to Otis, the only reason Dr. Blythe was not reporting Otis to the authorities is because he had lost his license to practice years ago, when he was sued for malpractice. Otis thought that it was his "money-making Dr. Blythe" act beneath the scope of his professional parameters, when in actuality, he was nothing short of a pseudo-charlatan. A man pretending to be something he no longer had the authority to be. Either way, Dr. Blythe could not report Otis to authorities because he would be implicating himself and again facing charges for practicing therapy with a suspended license.

As much as he wished he could report Otis, he just couldn't. He was also hoping that Otis would eventually be put away so he would no longer have to deal with him. Otis was drawing too much heat and had the potential to blow Dr. Blythe's entire operation wide open. He had been operating in obscurity with individuals like Otis for years and was doing quite fine. He wanted to keep it that way.

"Doc, right now, I am anxious and nervous about having to turn myself into jail. I just know that my mugshot will be all over the news, ruining my credibility." Otis was becoming nauseous at the thought.

Dr. Blythe could hardly stand it anymore. He understood why Otis was behaving the way he did with his cousin due to his history of childhood sexual abuse. But now that it was brought to his attention that he was a predator, he couldn't believe that Otis was only concerned about his reputation. Where was his empathy for his cousin? Although Dr. Blythe had lost his license, he was still an expert in the field of mental health and knew he was dealing with an extremely narcissistic sociopath.

"Okay. I see. Well, Otis, have you thought about facing the consequences of your actions at all? If so, how does that make you feel?" Dr. Blythe was attempting to help Otis understand how surface-level he was thinking by only being concerned with his reputation.

"Honestly, I know I won't be in jail long, and I am going to beat this case. My lawyer doesn't lose. The greatest blow I will suffer is the dirt on my name. It will be hard to shake."

"I understand, Otis. Have you been able to process what you shared with me the last session?"

Just as he asked the question, Dr. Blythe got a notification on his phone that his next client had arrived, which was the escape he was hoping for."

"Well, I wa—"

"You know what, Otis, my appointment just arrived. Can we pick this up another time?" Dr. Blythe insisted.

Otis could see Dr. Blythe was busy, so he decided to let him off the hook. "Sure thing, Doc. We'll talk later."

SIXTEEN

Jeston was back on the road from taking a day to rest, and recuperate after randomly encountering his mother, who had been giving him pure hell since he found her. According to his GPS he was thirty miles away from the treatment center in the middle of nowhere. Jeston was mentally defeated from dealing with his mother, who had now been talking shit to him for the last hour of the drive.

"Let me out of this damned car now, son! Who the hell do you think you are, kidnapping me?"

Jeston ignored her, as he gripped his wheel tighter silently wishing she would shut up. She was experiencing the beginning effects of withdrawals, which she had not allowed herself to feel for months.. It was heartbreaking to hear his mother speak to him in such a vile tone, but he knew this woman was not his mother. She was a cracked-out deadbeat. He just kept reminding himself of the good times when she was clean and sober, telling himself that was his real mother, that this lady in his car was a shadow of who she used to be and would return to her normal self once she was clean.

"Mama, I have to do this. You need help!" Jeston said calmly as she tried to get out of the moving car repeatedly by banging on the windows as if her frail arms could break them.

"You ain't shit, son! I knew I shouldn't have trusted you. Hell, you just like yo' damned daddy. No good nigga!" Laney was getting dope sick, a feeling she despised. She needed a fix, and she needed it now. But she couldn't escape this hell of a car ride she was in, which was adding to her sickness by making her nauseous.

"Let the damned window down now, Jeston! I mean it!" Laney needed to vomit, but Jeston was worried she would jump out of the car.

"No, Mama! Just chill. We are almost at the— AWWWW, SHIT!" Jeston yelled mid-sentence as his mother vomited all over his blood-red leather seats and custom dashboard. He was so disgusted that he came to a haltering stop right in the middle of the road. Jeston hopped out of the car, running around and opening his mother's door. Laney, who was too tired and dizzy to move, slowly leaned her thin body out of the car to finish her business whileJeston searched around in his trunk to see if he had anything to clean up her mess.

"Dammit, Mama, this is so sad. I can't believe you are in this state. I am so sick of you being a fuck-up!" Jeston had had enough and was experiencing the beginning of an inevitable and long overdue emotional break.

"You been fucking up my whole life. I can't take it anymore. Once I drop you off, I'm done with you! All this shit that's happening to Jainey is your fault too! You left her with Otis, and you knew he was a perv. All you care about is yourself. You're a selfish bitch, Mama!"

Jeston was so angry that he slipped and called his mother out of her name. He was ashamed, but it was too late to take it back. Besides, it's what he really felt. Lainey was in a daze and could not process what he was saying anyway, but she did hear him call her a bitch, and something about Otis hurting her baby girl, which shook her back to a fuzzy reality!

"Listen, son, I am still your mother. Don't you call me no bitch unless you ready to meet yo' maker! Wait, what did you say about my baby? What did he do to her?" Lainey really wanted to know. Her recent months long crack binge had made her forget about her daughters plight. She was still leaning over as Jeston cleaned around her in frustration with an old T-shirt.

"It doesn't matter; you can't help her anyway. You can't even help yourself. We are better off without you!" Jeston was full of anger, and having an in-depth conversation with his mother was moot. He wanted to get her out of his car as soon as possible. It was strange to him that he went from loving and idolizing his mother to hating her guts all in one lifetime. He didn't know if he could forgive her for what has happened to Jaines and for how she let herself go, he didn't care either. At the moment, he wanted her out of his sight. The last words he spoke to his mother broke her heart and silenced her.

They rode the rest of the way to the treatment center in the unbearable stench of Lainey's vomit and Jeston's heartache. After arriving at the treatment center, Jeston stayed with his mother long enough to give them a few details about her and check her in. Some of the workers helped him clean out his car with special chemicals made just for withdrawal throw-up, he figured.

Once his car was cleaned, he sped away without even saying goodbye. He was too hurt to speak another word to her and too angry to linger in her presence. Jeston was back on his mission, with his gun in his lap and one in the chamber with Otis's name on it!

———————————

After a long day of traveling Jaines and Angela had arrived back in her hometown, both full of nerves. Angela was scared to face her parents for the first time in so long; she did not know what emotions would arise and how she would handle them. She hadn't even seen her house since she was taken to the all-girls school as a seventeen-year-old pregnant girl, which was almost twenty years ago. The thought of being back there did not excite her in any way. She couldn't muster up a single good memory or happy thought except for rebelliously making love to her childhood sweetheart..

Jaines was unsure of another new place. Here she was again, being taken to another person's home. It seemed like all her life, she was being taken from here to there, never really belonging anywhere. *Who are these people?* she thought. She wondered why Angela never mentioned them until recently, why she never told any stories about her childhood. She suddenly realized she never even heard Angela mention her mother's or father's names.

"What do I call them?" Jaines curiously asked Angela as they turned the corner onto her parents' street.

"Um, call who?" Angela asked, confused by Jaines's question.

"Your parents. What are their names? You've never told me about them before."

Angela was pondering how to respond to Jaines as they came to a slow stopin front of her childhood home.. After a long silence, Angela explained to Jaines that she had a strained relationship with her parents but knows that she can trust them to take care of her until this trial is over. Angela assured Jaines not to worry and that no one would hurt her there.

"My parents were not the greatest people to me, Jaines, but I believe that time has taught them a very hard lesson. I know that they will do better for you. Just trust me. Oh, and just call them Mr. and Mrs Chambers for now."

Jaines was a ball of anxiety and just wanted to get into her new room and retreat to her safe place. She knew it wasn't the best place to go at a time like this, when she really needed to be brave enough to talk, but she was beginning to feel overwhelmed with emotions and worry.

After getting Jaines settled into one of the many guest rooms of parents' home, Angela agreed to sit down with her parents, but this wouldn't be the long-awaited reunion they had been hoping for. Angela was not happy or looking forward to rehashing old emotions about her childhood with these wretched people. . After all, she had moved on and made something great out of her life. And besides, the pain of her past was what really fueled her passion as a lawyer, and she often wondered would she be so good at it had it not been for all that they'd put herthrough.

"Angela, baby," her father said as his soft, raspy voice broke through the silent tension in the room. The three of them, Angela and her parents, were sitting in the library adjacent to the grand ballroom. As Angela sat directly across from her parents, she couldn't help but marvel at the beauty of their home. This home had been passed down to her father from his father; it had been in the family for generations. It was a marvelous mansion in the Hills.

Growing up, Angela's favorite part of the home was always the ballroom. Her parents hosted the most lavish parties and banquets, and occasionally, she would sneak in and peek at the lovely dresses and tuxedos their guests wore. She was almost having a happy memory until she heard her mother's voice yelling, "You better not be caught in my ballroom putting your nasty little fingerprints on my antiques, little girl!" Then, she remembered how particular her mother was about her things — way more particular about her things than she ever was about her.

"Baby, look. Your mother and I want to apologize about the way things were when you were with us," her father boldly interrupted her regrettable trip down memory lane. "We were young and ignorant, and really were only trying to give you the best."

"Really, Dad? The best?" The sound of her father's voice incensed Angela. She could not believe he had the audacity to say what they gave her was the best.

"Listen, Angela, we—" her mother began an attempt to interject on her father's behalf, but the sound of her mother's voice only added to Angela's fury.

"Mom, don't even start with me. I can't do this!" Angela

stood up and stormed for the door as her parents followed behind her, begging and pleading for her to stop. Angela was one foot out of the door when she heard the sweet sound of her name.

"Angela, wait!"

It was Jaines.

Angela stopped in her tracks turning only to see Jaines running through the foyer with her arms outstretched and her face soaked in tears. Before she knew it, Jaines was latched onto her waist holding her with all her might. Everything in Angela broke at that moment. Every grudge, every regret, every angry memory she had of her childhood broke. All she could feel was the depth of love flowing from Jaines's heart.

"Angela, please don't leave me. Everybody has left me. My mother. My granny. Jeston. I don't even know who my daddy is. Please don't leave me. Please, Angela," Jaines begged as she sobbed and melted into Angela's arms. Angela's parents stood and watched in the distance as Jaines and Angela slowly fell to the floor, both crying and embracing one another. Angela rocked Jaines back and forth as she cried, trying to soothe her sorrows.

"Angela, nobody in this world loves me like you. Nobody. I need you." Jaines pleaded.

Angela realized she couldn't leave Jaines there or anywhere else ever again.

Jeston had arrived back in Chicago still fuming, doing everything in his power to control his emotions. He knew he needed to clear his head so that he could find Otis and make him pay for hurting Jaines. Jeston was operating in a blind rage. He was pissed about his mother's condition, and the remnants of her vomit all over his custom interior. Pissed that he couldn't find his father, and that his sweet baby sister had been violated by someone he once aspired to be like.

Driving full-speed down a residential street, and completely zoned out, he was focused on one thing. During his unexpected detour with his mother, he had gotten a call from an informant stating that his cousin was on the news and was expected to be landing in Chicago soon to turn himself in to the police this evening. Jeston knew that if he was going to run into Otis, he needed to get there ahead of time and get in the right position. Jeston was so angry that he hadn't thought about any consequences or who this would hurt. All he could think about was making sure he aimed directly at Otis's head. Jeston pressed his foot on the gas harder as he sped down the block to the police station to await his cousin's arrival.

Back at the station, officers were preparing for the return of their local hometown hero. News reporters had just begun arriving on the scene hours before Otis's expected landing to prepare for live coverage of the most anticipated press conference the city had seen all year long. Stacy was at her the news station, gathering her documentation and preparing to arrive at the police department once she received word that Otis had landed.

Franco, Otis's lawyer, was had recently landed on his first-class flight from North Carolina to represent his client. He was fully confident in his plan of attack and ready to take Angela down.

But after receiving the details of the affidavit, Franco starting to feel something he hadn't felt since he first became a lawyer: emotions. He couldn't believe the allegations Otis was facing. He kept telling himself to just do his job, don't allow his heart any room. But he couldn't help it; he himself was a father of two precious baby girls that he would kill for. How could he possibly represent Otis if he was guilty? But he couldn't be guilty, right? The wrong outcome could ruin his reputation and credibility as a lawyer, and father.

He was starting to realize why Otis paid him the way he did. Perhaps he was a really bad man who knew it was only a matter of time before his shit started to bubble to the surface. Franco's head was spinning as he replayed his comments for the press conference briefing in his mind. He had become cold-hearted in his line of work because he learned that's the fastest way to be successful in his field, but this one was pricking his heart. He suddenly found himself doing something he hadn't done in decades. With his head bowed and eyes closed, he desperately prayed, seeking guidance from a trusted old friend.

"God, um, I'm so sorry I haven't come to You in so long, but today, I am troubled. God, please forgive me for all of my transgressions, and I hope You can hear me right now. I heard You don't listen to sinners like me. I know I'm not a good man, and I've done some pretty bad things for money. But God, I would never ever represent a man guilty of harming an innocent child in any way. You know me; I like drug dealers and money launderers. But this is beyond my realm of consciousness. Please, God, show me what to do and reveal to me the truth. In Jesus's name I pray, Amen."

SEVENTEEN

As the day grew later, and the night grew darker, Stacy and her crew loaded up the van and made their way to the police department to see the infamous money mogul.

She was excited for her first face-to-face encounter with the man she had just dropped a dime on. Although slightly intimidated by this being her first big story, and with the allegations beingso unbiblical; sheshe was struggling to believe them to be true. Still, she never knew Angela to lie, nevertheless on her own husband. And after meeting Jaines and experiencing the sweet innocence of her presence, her alliance had been made. She was committed to covering this story to its fullest extent while finding out who Otis was for herself. Her mission was to give the public the truth and give a voice to victims like Jaines!

Everyone at the station was on edge waiting for Otis. The Chief of Police had already prepared a special cell for him in protective custody, away from any of the local riffraff, in case he really had to book him. After all, he and Otis went way back, and Otis had helped the local police department on several occasions with its investments and trades to turn just enough profit to keep the doors open and the staff paid.

Chief Charles Andrews knew of Otis both personally and professionally and had already made up his mind that any little girl accusing him of what he had heard that affidavit alleged, even though he hadn't read it for himself, had to be out for a big payday. The Otis he knew was a stand-up guy who took care of his family and provided for his community. There was no way a man like him could ever hurt a child.

The chief wanted to make sure he provided the business mogul with the finest care until this entire thing blew over. In fact, he had already talked to the local bail bondsman, along with Otis's lawyer, to clear his bond. Little did the public know, Otis being booked was only a formality to please them. Chief Andrews had also already agreed to keep Otis's mugshot under lock and key and away from the public eye for as long as he could by advising the data entry clerks to not input Otis's data until he gave them the word to do so. If there was going to be a scandal in his city, he wanted to make sure his precinct's name was not slandered in the local gossip blogs. He knew that Otis was going to be cleared of these lies and wanted his precinct to reap any benefits it could from this process. Whatever he could do to protect the reputation of the great Chicago-bred Otis McGee was exactly what he was going to do!

Earlier that morning , Otis had landed in his private jet and was being escorted around Chicago in his luxury Rolls-Royce by his personal driver. After a day of making secret appearances with local counsel members, and business owners he was finally headed towards the police station, when he was suddenly flushed with emotions and becamesick to his stomach.

"Hey! Pull over! Hurry up, man!"

His driver quickly obeyed, pulling over to the side of the road while Otis rushed out of the vehicle to vomit. He didn't know why he was sick; he hadn't been able to eat since all of this broke. Perhaps it was the guilt of his sin breaking free — or the reality that he was a monster was too much for him to bear. It definitely wasn't fear of incarceration; he was confident in that. He knew his attorney and his friends at the police station had already made sure he would be in and out. Maybe it was the fear of the unknown. As much as Otis felt like his money and power had always gotten him out of a jam before, this time he was worried and did not know how this would end.

"Okay, man. I'm good. Let's go," Otis reassured his driver as they pulled away to continue towards the police station. The closer they got the station, the more he began to realize the weight of his actions and how he really had hurt his cousin. He kept thinking was, *But I was just showing her love.*

However, he knew that wasn't the love she deserved, and neither did he when he was a child. He wrestled with his emotions and refused to accept or ever say that he was a pedophile!

How can I be a pedophile? I'm Otis McGee! he thought to himself.

But deep down, he knew the truth. He needed to talk to someone who could help him understand the nature of who he was and why he was such a twisted individual.

"Hello? Who is this?"

"Hey, Pops. It's me, Otis." With a single phone call, he

resurrected an era of his life he had so desperately tried to keep buried under ambition, overachievement, and success.

"Son, is that you? Oh, my boy!" Otis could hear the age in his father's voice, which sounded raspy and faint, as if the years of life had stolen his vibrato.

"Yes, Dad. It's so good to hear your voice."

Otis hadn't spoken to his dad in the many years since he had left home. It wasn't that he disowned his father, but his father reminded him of a bitter beginning, one he had spent his entire life trying to forget. He thought he loved his father and appreciated how much his father fought for him throughout his childhood, but he also resented him for his favoritism that cost him the comradery of his brothers and the sanity of his mother. Because of his father's partiality towards him, he was left alone to fend for himself. After a few minutes of superficial chatter, Otis had had enough of the formalities; it was time to get to the basis of his call.

"Listen, Dad. I am really experiencing a lot right now, and I need you to help me understand things."

"Okay, son."

"Dad, please tell me the truth. Why did you love me so much more than my brothers?"

Otis was completely unaware of how unprepared he was for his father's truth.

"Well, son, I never wanted to have to be the one to tell you this, but I think it's time."

His father proceeded to tell him that when he met his mother, she was a street worker who had lived a hard life. She was abandoned at a young age by her mother and became a ward of the state; when she aged out of the system, she had no family and no plan. She was soon picked up by a local madam and groomed into a life of sex work. By the time he had met her, she was tired and wanted to get out of the life. But she had five young children already, all by different men, some she knew and others just clients. She was in a desperate state, but he loved her. There was something about her he couldn't ignore.

He agreed to marry her despite her condition, and they relocated and started a new life. Throughout the relationship, he kept pressing her for a son of his own, with his own DNA. But she was worn down, and her body had suffered many traumas, which made them give up. Until one day when they found out she was pregnant! It was a miracle. He told Otis how he prayed every day of the pregnancy that he would be a boy, and on the day she gave birth, it was the happiest day of his life. He had his very own son! Right away, Otis had become the apple of their eyes, the result of true love. He represented hope for his mother and father, and redemption. They felt like God gave them a new story with Otis, one that was right and organized.

Otis was in shock by his mother's history and the fact that none of his brothers were his full-blooded brothers. It all made sense now, why his parents treated him so much better.

"But Daddy, the way you treated me made my brothers hate me. I lost my whole family because you and Mama couldn't be fair."

"Oh, Otis, them boys was rotten before I ever got to them. They was all raised in a whore house. Your mama gave up on them before I met her. I ain't saying it's right, but you was never gonna need them anyway!"

Otis wept in disbelief of his father's cold-heartedness.

"Listen, Dad. I am a monster, okay?! This is all your fault! If I had never gone to foster care, this would have never happened to me! I hate you!"

"I knew it. I knew you wasn't right the day I came and seen you at that damn building. That's why I stole you back! What did they do to you, son?! You tell me wha—"

Click!!! Otis couldn't take anymore! He hung up the phone. His father couldn't help him anyway. As far as he was concerned, he would be a normal person if his father hadn't have been so selfish! Somebody had to take the blame for this, and Otis would be sure it wouldn't be himself.

"You're dead to me," he whispered to himself while simultaneously blocking his father's number as they continued toward the station.

As Otis's driver stopped in the back of the station, he was greeted by his lawyer standing by , waiting to brief him. Franco walked over to the driver's side of the vehicle and advised the driver to stay put, that this would be over really soon, and that Otis will not be staying overnight. Franco then jumped inside to give Otis the rundown on how this night would play out.

"Lots of reporters are already here. Don't be alarmed. Word spread fast. Once you're inside, you will be photographed and fingerprinted. Your bond is already paid, so you'll be in and out."

So far, Otis was pleased.

"But there are a few conditions we must meet. One: You have to wear an ankle monitor until trial and follow those stipulations, and two: We have to do the press conference. But you don't have to speak. I'm actually advising you not to speak."

Otis's mind was racing, and he was still sitting in the emotions of the phone call with his father. He didn't have the mental capacity to argue with any conditions that didn't require him to be held overnight.

"Okay. Let's do this. I'm ready," Otis agreed.

Franco could feel Otis's energy and knew he was different. Something was off, but now wasn't the time to ask. Franco was ready to get this formality over with so he could really get to the truth.

Once inside the police station, Otis was greeted by his good friend, the chief, who hurried him through processing and ordered everyone not to speak to Otis about anything. After he was fingerprinted, he was swept into a processing room, where an officer affixed his ankle monitor and went over the procedures with him. Otis found out he would be confined to the home of his choosing until trial. However, it had to be in the United States. Otis chose to stay in his ranch in North Carolina; he figured he'd leave the mansion to his wife for the moment until this was all said and done. He could not go further than fifty feet from the residence unless approved by the judge. Due to his status and a substantial donation under the table to the city's attorney general , he was able to skip his initial court date. Money had the power make one blind to conflicts of interest, the prohibition of bribery, and even the unlawful acceptance of funds. Otis, didn't care about any of that anyways; All he had to do was agree, which he did.

Patrons of the police department couldn't help but be

captivated by Otis's presence. He was a tall, caramel-toned, lean, physically fit brother who walked with grace. All of the women looked upon him with desire, and the men with admiration. Otis was a star; he shined without effort. He looked so good on the exterior, but inside he knew he was a broken and ugly man. Too much of a coward to face his truth and accept responsibility for his actions. He had already decided he wasn't going down for this; he wasn't going to lose his life's work for this. He was committed to his lies and prepared to take the truth to his grave.

After his ankle monitor was in place, Otis was escorted by the chief and his lawyer to the front of the police station, where reporters were waiting to ask questions.

"Hold on, Otis." Franco abruptly stopped mid-stride. "Listen. Do not speak. I don't care what they say; you let me handle it," he said firmly before they entered onto the front steps of the station, making solid eye contact with Otis to confirm he understood.

As the front door swung open, they were all blinded by the lights of flashing cameras and stunned at the sound of Otis's name being called.

"Otis, is it true that you raped and tortured your own cousin?"

"Otis, are you a pedophile?"

"Otis, are the things in the affidavit true?"

"Otis, what do you have to say about the accusations being brought against you?"

"Otis! Otis! Otis!"

It seemed like reporters from every news station and media

outlet in the world were present and thirsty for any answers they could get. For the first time in his adult life, Otis did not like the spotlight shining so closely on him.

Stacy Whittaker and her crew had positioned themselves right in front of the podium, in direct alignment with Otis. Excitement spilling over, she couldn't believe she was close enough and touch him if she wanted. He didn't know her right then, but she was determined to make sure that after that night, he would never forget her.

Jeston had arrived at the scene just in time to catch the press conference. He had fire in his eyes and ice in his veins. He knew what he had to do. Moments later Franco approached the microphone to open the floor for questions.

"Good evening, Chicago. I am sure you have all heard the allegations being made about my client. Keep in mind that my client is innocent until proven guilty in a court of law. The court of public opinion pales in comparison to tangible evidence. Therefore, we will only be taking a few questions."

Stacy burst forward with authority in her inflection, making sure she was seen and heard.

"Mr. Beezy, is it true that your client has paid affiliates within the police department working on his behalf?!"

Franco was struck by Stacy's beauty, making notice of her right away. But he laughed off her question arrogantly.

"Ha! I refuse to entertain such nonsense! Next questi—"

Before he could even finish, Stacy burst forth with another.

"Then how do you explain the fact that he just arrived in the back of the station less than an hour ago and has already been fully processed? Did he have a pre-trial hearing? Why does he already have an ankle monitor?"

Members of the media were mumbling and taking notes rapidly as they looked on in suspense, awaiting an answer. Meanwhile, Otis, Franco, and the police chief were all stunned at her accuracy. They wanted to know who this woman was.

"I'm sorry, who are you?" Franco asked.

"Stacy Whittaker, Channel 26 News Now. Do you care to answer my questions, or are you too busy wondering who I am?"

Everyone was quiet in suspense as the situation unfolded. These were brand-new allegations of police corruption to add to the sexual abuse.

"Ma'am, forgive my pause. I am shocked that you would make such a bold statement against the prestigious Chicago Police Department. However, your claims hold no validity, and I can assure you that my client proceeded with the same due process as every law-abiding citizen of this country who has been accused of a crime."

Franco stepped back away from the microphone for a second and whispered to the chief and Otis that he was ready to wrap it up if they were in agreement. Franco was prepared for questions about the case with Jaines, but this fiery stranger just threw a curveball.

Jeston, who was standing about thirty feet in the back of the crowd, positioned himself directly in front of Otis and aimed his weapon inconspicuously. In the dark of the night, he was hidden by the obscurity of his all black with his hoodie, which he tied tight around his face. Jeston was furiously gripping the gun with all his strength, sweat beading on his forehead, with both hands on the handle. He swiftly removed the safety. firmly pressing his finger on the trigger, when suddenly Stacy burst forward again, this time jumping up on the tips of her toes just enough to block Jeston's shot!

He froze, his trigger finger paused mid-squeeze!

The feisty reporter yelled out her final question. "Excuse me, sir! Have you any knowledge of the whereabouts of your only nephew, Jeston McGee?! We would love to hear his side of the story!"

The sound of his own name shook Jeston back to reality. He suddenly lowered his weapon, in disbelief over what he was about to do!

"Shit, man, I'm tripping!" Jeston said softly to himself as he tucked his revolver away in his pocket and fled the scene of his intended crime.

EIGHTEEN

It had been three days since the press conference, and the media was still in an uproar with the recent release of Otis's mugshot. There was little the chief could do to hold off on releasing them since the probing of one nosey little reporter. Stacy Whittaker's questioning of Otis and his team during the press conference had created enough speculation to cause an internal investigation into how he was processed. The chief's intentions to help his long-time finance buddy was potentially going to backfire.

While the police department was dealing with its unexpected probing, Stacy was basking in the ambiance of her newfound fame. Everyone was talking about the pretty little spitfire who not only was the first to break the story about Otis but who also boldly accused the Chicago police of showing favoritism and not following protocol. Her tactic had worked out just like she wanted it to. Her goal was to create enough buzz around her name to earn some clout with Otis's inner circle. She was hoping to slide her way into his inner courts and eventually to him to get an inside scoop on the business mogul's life story. She had already scheduled a meeting with Jaines and Angela for later in the week to get a detailed description of how things went down. She was also hoping to find out where the missing nephew was in all of this. Once she had all the pieces to the puzzle, she planned to drop a bomb on Otis and let the world know who he really was.

Back at her parents' estate, Angela had already enlisted the help of a world-renowned psychotherapist to help Jaines process her trauma and prepare her for trial. She knew that Jaines would have to take the stand, and she would have to be sharp and hold up under pressure. While Jaines was spending time in therapy, Angela was actively avoiding her parents as she worked with the Chicago police department to gather evidence for court. She herself was amid the greatest emotional trial she had experienced since her baby was snatched from her arms as a teen. Not only was she back in the home she hated with the parents she despised. She found herself needing them, which she hated even more. She needed them to look after Jaines, and this was truly the calmest environment for them both right now.

Angela was finding it hard to continue ignoring her emotions; she hadn't quite sat with the truth that her husband was sexually violating her sweet little Jaines and that she was going to face him in court. All in one day, her fairy tale life ended, and the hardest part was that the love of her life turned out to be someone she no longer knew. She was devastated and embarrassed. She too had a reputation as a prosecutor that was polished and unmatched. But what would the world think of her now? What would they say? She couldn't process it all; she had to keep pushing it to the back of her mind so she could focus on Jaines. Jaines needed her more. Her own heart would have to wait.

"Hello? Jeston?! Jeston, where are you?" Angela was on her way to the law library to do some research when she got a call from her nephew.

"Hey, Ang. I'm at home." Jeston was standing shirtless, looking out his bedroom window at the Chicago skyline.

"You okay? How's your mom?

"My mom is fine. I took her to the rehab facility. Listen, I need to talk to you." Jeston was overwhelmed with emotions and falling apart over the recent circumstances. He was still angry with Otis and afraid of what he might do.

"What's wrong, J?" Angela inquired.

"I can't be alone right now. I might do something stupid," he said with desperation in his voice. He was hoping she would read between the lines and bail him out so he wouldn't have to humble himself and ask for help, something life had trained him never to do.

"Okay. As soon as we hang up, I'll book you a flight here. Call me when you get to the airport. I'll send the ticket info in five minutes." Angela was in full-on mother mode! She saw Jaines and Jeston as her own, and she would do anything they needed her to do without hesitation.

"Thank you, Ang. I'll see you soon!"

Jeston ended the call with tears in his eyes. He could not believe that he needed someone, and they were there. That he could call for help, and help would come. He was grateful and relieved that for once in his life, he would not have to figure this one out on his own!

NINETEEN

Six months had passed since the infamous press conference, and the fire around Otis McGee was still ravenously burning. The public had not forgotten, nor would they excuse the allegations against him. How could somebody they had trusted so much be accused of such filth? How did his wife not know? How could the cousin allow him to abuse her for so long and never tell? Was she telling the truth? There were so many questions as the entire city of Chicago and abroad prepared themselves to watch the most scandalous trial of the decade.

Back at the rehab facility, Lainey was preparing for discharge after six months of successful treatment and aftercare. She had been sober. Her mind was clear, but her heart was broken. Even though she had experienced several intense therapy sessions as a part of her treatment, it was hard for her to accept that she had abandoned her children and let her life go to shit at the hands of crack cocaine. Today was her last day at the facility, and she was waiting for someone in her family to answer her call. If she couldn't get a ride out of there, she would have to stay longer, which she desperately did not want to do.

"Hello? Jeston?"

Jeston was just waking up to the smell of coffee and bacon coming from the kitchen of Angela's parents' home. He had decided to stay there with Jaines to support her as she prepared for trial.

"Yeah, Ma, how are you?" he said to his mother, who was in a bit of a panic on the other line.

"I'm doing just fine, baby. I just need a ride from the facility. You think you can come pick me up today?"

With all the mayhem from the recent revelations with Jaines, Jeston had completely forgotten about his mother. He had made the decision the day he left her there that he would never look back. That he was tired of her toxic abuse cycle. That she was on her own.

"I'm sorry, Mama, but I can't come pick you up. I am here at Angela's with Jaines. She needs me right now. You will have to find another way."

Click. He hung up.

Lainey was in disbelief that her baby boy was so cold. But in her sober-minded state, she fully understood why. She accepted she had to do this by herself.

After speaking with her treatment coordinator, Lainey learned there was a sober living community in North Carolina where she used to live and that she would be able to transfer there once all the paperwork was completed. Supposedly, it would be only a few more days until she was transferred. Lainey also had already been given the contact information for her new treatment coordinator, who she had heard was "the best of the best." Although she wanted to be with her children so she could apologize and work on healing, she knew this was the smartest way to do it. She would have to work hard and get back on her feet and show them that this time was different.. She would have to work her way back into their hearts one step at a time.

———————

Angela had been working tirelessly to build her case against her husband. She even decided to hand the case over to new representatives to avoid the obvious conflict of interest. However, she was still leading the case and spoonfeeding the new lead prosecutor all the details. The new prosecutor was Charles Bluett, someone she graduated from law school with and whom she could trust. Charles and Angela had similar track records and were known as winners amongst their colleagues. He had only lost two cases in his twenty-year career. He had been fully briefed and was ready for trial which was swiftly approaching.

In just a short thirty days, the long-awaited moment of truth would finally arrive. In her time preparing for trial, Angela was traveling back and forth to North Carolina to interview potential witnesses. She was looking for someone who would not be afraid to take the stand against Otis. So far, she was able to secure Jaines's cheer coach, Andre, and Jaines's best friend Elizaveth. Elizaveth's mother vehemently refused for weeks until she had a heart-to-heart with Jaines, who urged her to allow her daughter to testify, that she needed her, that she was one of her biggest weapons in the case. That without her, she had no other witnesses to her abuse.

Unfortunately, Angela was unable to secure any other

personal witnesses; everyone else would be professional. She had already heard through the grapevine that Otis had a full lineup of personal and professional witnesses for the case and was telling people that it was already over before it started. His team had already started a full slander campaign on Jaines and her family, exposing her troubled childhood and drug-addicted mother. Social media was in a frenzy over how "Saint Otis," who was kind enough to take in his poor, abandoned cousin, was now being falsely accused of sexual abuse by the little misfit. Otis's slandering was a sneak attack, but Angela was unphased.

Back at his ranch in rural North Carolina, Otis had been waiting patiently as Franco continued to prepare for trial. He had been surprised at how well things were still going for him. So far since the allegations had come out against him, he only lost three major clients, which hardly put a dent in his annual revenue. He was still worth millions and still had the majority of his major contracts. In fact, since all of the drama leaked to the media, more companies have taken an interest in working with his finance firm, and overseas accounts had tripled. He was making more money now than he ever had before.

Otis was, however, struggling emotionally and mentally. His therapist had blocked him and ceased all contact. Otis was sure he was working with Angela at this point. Angela was his closest family member, and he could not confide in anyone because then they would know he was actually guilty. He was lonely and missed his family. He missed his wife and was devastated at how things had turned out. A few weeks after pressing charges, Angela filed for divorce; she didn't ask for anything in the settlement and refused to keep the estate Otis tried to leave her. She left it all to Otis, the house and all his millions.

Angela had the divorce case expedited, and it was recently made final. They hadn't spoken to one another in months. Otis never once thought that Jaines would ever act out; he thought he had it all under control. He was confident that he had her mind and body, and she would never tell a soul what he was doing to her. Being in the place he was in life came as an unexpected surprise to him. Because of his behavior, he had lost almost all of the things that were significant to him. So far, he was able to keep what mattered the most: his reputation, and soon he would go to trial and be proven innocent, the truth didn't matter anymore. Otis had buried it deep within, and was prepared to continue his façade. Besides he always came out on top, this case would be no different Soon a jury of his peers would prove what he already believed, he was not a monster, not a pedophile. Simply a man who gave a chance to an ungrateful, ghetto, gold digging little brat. Yeah, it had already been curated, and the public had already eaten it up!

TWENTY

Angela, sleepily stretched beneath her heavy duvet, pushing out her arms and legs, basking in the sound and sensation of her muscles extending and her joints popping as she awakened to the shriek of her phone's ringtone blaring in her ear. It was the middle of the morning in Johannesburg, and she was still recovering from a long night of dancing and drinking with Jaines and the locals as they celebrated the grand opening of her advocacy center.

Wondering who could be calling at this hour, she reluctantly picked up the phone.

"Hello…?" she said hoarsely, with the sound of sleep radiating from her vocal chords. "Who is this?"

"Angela, it's Franko."

"Wait, who? Why are you calling me?"

"It's about Otis."

"I don't care about Otis. Please do not call me again!"

She ended the call and slammed the phone down on the bed beside her.

Ping! The sound of the text notification fueled her uninvited frustration.

Angela, please hear me out.

You will want to hear this.

You need to hear this.

Franko texted persistently, insisting that Angela give him a chance to speak to her. He caught her in the vulnerable hours of the morning, mid-hangover, and her defenses were down. Angela did not have the energy to be stubborn. She reluctantly pushed redial and shoved her phone to her ear.

"What is it now? she insisted with as much attitude as she could muster up.

"Angela, Otis is … He's dead."

Angela suddenly shot up in her bed, those words being an instant remedy from her drunken night, forcing her to become fully alert and completely coherent.

"What? He's dead?" she asked in a panic. The trial had been ugly, the outcome even more so. She and Jaines had moved as far away from North Carolina and Chicago as they could to escape the harsh realities Otis left in his path of injustice. Although she hated what they had become, she still held the memories of what she thought they once were. Tears began to fall from her eyes as she took a quick leap down memory lane; she couldn't believe the culprit of Jaines's nightmare finally met the fate he truly deserved.

"The incident is still being investigated, but he was found by his housemaid yesterday morning. She was doing her routine cleaning when she noticed that he hadn't gotten up for breakfast. She went to check on him in his bedroom and found him slumped over at his desk. That's all I know right now."

"Oh my goodness, this is unbelievable. I mean, I just … I'm at a loss for words."

"Listen, there is one more thing," Franco interrupted her silence. "He left a letter. It's in a sealed envelope; it said "For Jaines's Eyes Only."

"What?! No. Absolutely not! Who has the letter?" Angela insisted.

"Right now, the police have it, but soon I will have it. I am his acting attorney, and I am legally obligated to carry out my client's last wishes, Angela. You know that."

"Given the nature of the circumstances between them, I believe his wishes are irrelevant, and the letter should be destroyed! Jaines is a victim — *his* victim. I won't have it. Burn the letter," Angela demanded as she fumed with disgust at the thought of Otis's final words to Jaines. *What could he possibly have to say to her?* He left her in the thralls of a scandal that she had to leave the country to seek solace from. As far as Angela was concerned, whatever he had to say was bullshit and needed to be buried with him.

"Angela, I know this is hard for you, but whether you like it or not, the letter may be released to the public at some point during this process. It's better for her to see it before the world does," Franco suggested as he abruptly ended the call.

Angela was enraged and consumed with emotions, not to mention the alcohol in her liver and kidneys had yet to filter out of her bloodstream. It was too much to process at the moment. She fell back into her bed, shoving her covers over her head with frustration, screaming at the top of her lungs.

Back in North Carolina, Franco was left with the task of handling Otis's affairs in the wake of his sudden departure. Since the trial ended, Franco had a new outlook on himself and his business practices. Otis was the lesson in disguise he never saw coming; it was humbling and unfortunate how it all ended. He knew the outcome was unfair for Jaines and felt helpless to do anything to help her without discrediting himself as a lawman. He had recently ended the call with the police, who advised him of the nature of Otis's untimely demise, which at the moment appeared to be self-inflicted with no evidence of foul play.

Forensic investigators had already broken the seal on his letter to Jaines to determine if it was associated with any motive, and it was. But the letter wasn't his business; it didn't belong to him, and he had already committed to never reading it. His only obligation was to get the letter to its intended target, eighteen-year-old Leola Jaines McGee.

Franco began the business of preparing his statement for the public, which he knew would be coming as soon as the authorities finalized notifying the next of kin. Franco was in the middle of his vacation with his family when he got the call from the Chicago Police Chief to inform him of the news. Right away, he didn't know how to feel, but he surely did not feel sorrow for Oits. After representing Otis, Franco decided to take a break from the business. He had earned enough money to retire if he wanted, but he liked the thrill of chasing a win. In this case, however, Otis did not deserve to win. He was, in fact, guilty of what he was accused of: molesting and sexually assaulting his own flesh and blood, trapping her in her room, torturing her with emotional manipulation for years, stealing her childhood from her, and framing his actions as love. He was the monster Jaines did her best to prove him to be.

Her best, however, wasn't enough against Franco and his ego, his determination to be victorious at all costs. The same determination that left him feeling low and like less of a man. During the trial, he couldn't see that he was in too deep; he knew Otis was guilty, but he couldn't let his guilt be associated with him and what he had built for himself. He fought to prove reasonable doubt, which was unfortunately easy, given Jaines's family history. The outcome exposed to Franco that he was morally corrupt; he had gained the world and lost his soul. Representing Otis revealed an error in him, one that he was now eager to edify.

It had been almost two years since Otis's sensational trial, one that led Franco back to the altar, seeking repentance and forgiveness for his wrongdoings. He had decided that he would now dedicate his work to victim's advocacy to somehow honor Jaines and how he wronged her. He was happy Otis was dead, and once he settled all of his affairs, this would be the last time he would ever think of him.

———————

Johannesburg had been an asylum for Jaines and Angela, and they had been thriving since their arrival. Jaines was waking up from a long night of drinking and partying with Angela. She wasn't used to alcohol, and this was the first time Angela had ever let her partake. Jaines herself couldn't believe she was imbibing. She loathed the taste of it but loved the burn as it traveled down her throat and how loose it made her feel. Throughout her life, she had felt invisible and scared to speak. But last night, she was powerful. She felt brave as she danced with the locals and celebrated her cousin's new accomplishments. But nobody told her that in less than twenty-four hours, she would pay severely for this liquid courage.

"Angela, my stomach hurts so bad," Jaines moaned as she stumbled into Angela's suite and plunged herself onto her California king bed. "Why did you let me drink so much?" she complained to her half-asleep cousin.

"I'm sorry, baby girl. I just wanted you to loosen up and have a good time," Angela mumbled with her eyes closed as they both abruptly burst into laughter at the thought of Jaines tipsily prancing around the dance floor.

"I've never seen you move like that, girl!" Angela chuckled.

"I've never seen me move like that, either," Jaines laughed as they both lay in the bed flat on their backs, staring at the ceiling.

"I just want you to be okay here, Jaines. Are you okay?"

"I am still finding that out, but I think I will be." Jaines was still massaging her belly and staring at the ceiling as she thought about her life and if she would really be okay. The trial was hard, and she was upset that she lost when she was being completely honest. The injustice of the system made her lose faith in the American legal system; it was a brutal lesson to learn at such a young age, but so far, her entire life had been brutal.

"I think the therapy was good. I can think more clearly now. But the alcohol on the other hand, not so good," Jaines stated as she and Angela laughed and both rolled over simultaneously to face each other.

Angela knew she had to break the news to Jaines that Otis had died and left her a letter. She was a firm believer in ripping the Band-Aid off and getting on with life. No need to delay the inevitable, but with Jaines, she always took a softer approach.

"Listen, baby girl. I have something to tell you. It's about Otis. Would you like for me to tell you now, later, or not at all?"

The sound of Otis's name always made Jaines sick to her stomach and threw her into an unwanted trip down memory lane. His abuse was still fresh in her brain and left neurological scars. She could still feel his touch on her skin. She had been hoping that somatic therapy would help ease this displeasure, but she also frequently reminded herself that hoping was still meaningless. Angela had taught her to face life, to face reality, not to run from the hard stuff. The trial had empowered her to use her voice and tell her truth. unafraid of the outcome. She was ready for this, whatever it was. She was ready.

"Tell me now," Jaines said with confidence that she could handle what was coming her way.

Angela took a deep breath and a long exhale. "No easy way to say this, my love, but Otis has passed away," she said softly, looking Jaines in the eyes to carefully gauge her reaction.

Jaines was stoic, the words still echoing in her head. She couldn't believe what she'd just heard. Her heart was pounding, and she was filled with a range of emotions. Good, bad, and indifferent.

"Jaines, baby, are you okay?" Angela asked while softly rubbing her arm.

"Um-hmm." She shook her head.

"Okay. Do you have any words for how you feel?"

Jaines couldn't speak. She shook her head no.

She sat up in the bed and dropped her head into her hands, overwhelmed with thoughts and feelings. Perhaps she wasn't ready.

"Baby girl, there is one more thing I need to tell you. Would you like for me to tell you now, or do you need more time?" Angela asked softly as she slowly sat up in the bed next to a tearful Jaines.

"Tell me now," Jaines said, thinking she might as well get it over with.

"Okay, my love," Angela stated softly before she continued. "There is a letter; he left it for you. But you don't have to read it if you don't want to."

Jaines abruptly shot up to her feet and ran from Angela's room. Hearing this was too much for her to process. Angela did not chase her; she had learned to let Jaines be alone while she processed deep emotions, giving her space to come to her own conclusions, something the family therapist taught them during trial preparation.

"What a fucking morning," Angela mumbled underneath her breath as she got out of bed to start her day.

———————————

Franco was annoyed that Otis had found a way to make him do his dirty work even while dead. Tropical palm trees blew in the cool breeze as he sat beachside, Chromebook in one hand and a Long Island iced tea in the other. He was frustrated with the current news of Otis's death because he knew it meant pulling old skeletons out of the closet. The trial was a nightmare for everyone involved, and Franco knew the entire spectacle would soon be circulating again, especially when Stacy Whittaker and her greedy-for-gossip news crew found out.

Franco reclined back in his lounge chair as he cracked open his computer to pull up Otis's last will and testament. Franco wanted to finalize the affairs of his estate expeditiously. As he browsed through Otis's legal documents, he had a sudden realization that it would have made sense for Otis to change his will post-divorce, but he hadn't. At least, not that he was aware of. This would turn into a legal disaster for Franco if he had missed that detail. Otis was a millionaire and owned several international businesses, homes, planes, cars, etc. He had several financial accounts both locally and overseas. The last he'd checked, Otis had left entire fortune to his wife and was expected to make her the sole heir. Otis had the authority to access his legal documents and make changes at any time, but he was always supposed to notify Franco. Franco just realized that it had been years since he last checked or updated any of his paperwork.

"Otis, you sneaky S.O.B.," he mumbled to himself as he frantically searched his legal files to locate his Will. Once Franco found the will, he quickly jumped to the paragraph that listed beneficiaries.

"Ugh", Franco sighed in disbelief while throwing his head back on his chair. He could not believe what he was seeing. How could this have gotten past him? It was too late to change it; the damage was done! There was only one thing left to do!

Angela's phone rang. Frustrated, she answered it.

"Seriously? Stop calling me, Franco."

"Angela! Drop the dramatics. Trust me, we need to talk!"

TWENTY-ONE

It had been three days since the news broke that the infamous Otis McGee had died. The authorities had yet to release the cause of death. The public was on the tips of its toes as they waited to hear the latest details in the story. Stacy Whittaker and her team had been in touch with Angela for exclusive information, but Angela was refusing to speak to the public anymore about anything pertaining to her ex-husband, and she fiercely shielded Jaines from all media inquisitions.

"Good morning, Chicago. I am Stacy Whittaker, and you are watching Channel 26 News Now. Thank you for joining me for the latest details on the premature death of Chicago's very own Otis McGee. It's been three days since he was discovered unresponsive in his home; however, authorities have yet to release any additional details about the cause of death. As you may know, Otis McGee was just at the center of a notorious trial a little over two years ago in which he was acquitted on all charges of sexual abuse against a teenaged victim. The victim was later revealed to be his younger cousin, Jaines McGee. The McGee family has not spoken on his death and has requested privacy during this time. Stay tuned for the latest on this story; we'll have more details as they develop."

––––––––––

The morning dew was settled firmly on the beds of the leaves as the sun crept up above the horizon. Africa had the most beautiful sunrises and sunsets, and Angela loved the smell of the fresh morning air in Johannesburg. The tea in her cup was still steaming as she sat down on her patio to admire the artistry of the morning sky. Being in South Africa had been a blessing for her and Jaines; it was a perfect launching pad for her advocacy center, which she affectionately named Leola's Corner: A Center for Women and Children. It was a necessary escape from the madness in North Carolina. She hadn't planned on leaving the States, but the weight of the trial had been too much on her and Jaines, and the outcome was the final nail in the coffin. *How could Otis win? How could Franco represent him when he knew he was guilty? How was the physical evidence not enough to convict him?*

Angela knew the answers. This was not a question of guilt; this was a battle of power and status. Jaines had no status, no power, and her only claim to any sort of wealth was Otis, which Franco used against her. Her heart broke for Jaines, to see all she had to endure during the trial only to be seen as a liar and a gold digger. At the time, leaving the country was the only way for them to flee the brutal insistence of their guilt in social media. With the verdict, Jaines and Angela became social pariahs and could not go anywhere without being harassed by paparazzi or berated by strangers in public.

"Jaines, is it true that you made the whole thing up?"

"Did you lie on your cousin to get money?"

"Why would you tell a lie on the only person who helped you?"

"Angela, were you in on this? Did you set up your husband?"

It was exhausting and unfair. Thankfully in their small tucked away town in Africa, they were everyday people. Nobody knew them, and no one cared about their past. It was a new beginning, an opportunity for Jaines to create the life she wanted and deserved. Angela was also thriving with her legal expertise, and her passion for helping marginalized populations coupled well with her financial resources.

As soon as her feet hit the ground, she went to work researching the area of greatest need, which proved to be women's advocacy. It was all-encompassing; women needed a voice, resources, and education. They needed community and help finding greater independence. She loved what she was doing there, and Jaines was getting stronger every day, becoming more vocal about her needs and branching out at the local university. Life was good again, until she got the news of Otis's death.

It had been less than a week since Franco interrupted her drunken slumber with the news of Otis's death, and Angela's emotions were in complete disarray. One moment she hated him, the next she felt sorry for him, then the next she was angry again. Jaines wasn't doing any better; she hadn't left her room in three days and refused to talk. Angela knew she would have to break her silence soon. It was the crack of dawn, and she was sitting with her thoughts as she waited for Franco's call. She had been avoiding him all week, but he was adamant that she needed to hear what he had to say.

Her phone rang, breaking her out of her thoughts.

"What is it, Franco?" she demanded angrily.

"Listen, Angela. I deserve the hatred you have for me; I really do. But let's try to set it aside for a moment to discuss this. You need to be clear-headed to process what I am about to tell you," Franco insisted softly, trying to settle Angela's nerves.

"Fine. Get on with it."

"I spoke with the detectives; I know the cause of death. I also have the letter."

"How did he die? Did someone poison the dirtbag?"

"Self-inflicted gunshot wound to the chest," Franco stated matter-of-factly.

"What a coward," Angela stated without remorse.

"Listen, he died by suicide to avoid facing the backlash from the truth he revealed in his letter to Jaines."

"Wait, you read the letter?"

"Hell no, and I never will. The detectives told me it was where they found the motive," Franco stated.

"Well, what was the motive?" Angela inquired.

"His guilt. Apparently, the letter is an admission of his guilt."

"I fucking hate him!" Angela shouted. "He still finds a way to control the narrative. He's disgusting to me. We don't want that letter, Franco."

"Angela, I am sorry, but that is not your decision to make. Jaines is eighteen now. The choice is hers," Franco reminded her firmly.

"Whatever! She doesn't want it, trust me," Angela insisted.

"Angela, there is something else …"

"I really don't think I can take anything else," she expressed, the sound of defeat in her voice.

"I know, and I am so sorry, but Otis changed his will. He left everything to Jaines. I mean everything. Every dollar, every property, every business, it's all hers."

Angela was immediately sick to her stomach and abruptly ended the call to run to the bathroom and release her vomit, her mind reeling at the nerve of Otis to leave his fortune to his victim. Jaines only ever wanted justice!

———————————

Unbelievably, the narcissist continued to win.

Jaines hadn't spoken a single word since the news of Otis's death emerged. She was overwhelmed with emotions and could not properly express them. She could not organize them. She had only just begun to express herself through the help of therapy and had not mastered the art of processing so many thoughts and feelings all at once. On the surface, she seemed sad, but internally, she was satisfied. Justice had been served to her by some power higher than her previous American injustice. God heard her prayers, and Otis had met his demise. He did not deserve to continue to live and prosper after what he had done to her.

But how did he die? she wondered as she sat on the sofa bed, gazing out of the window at the beautiful sunrise. She wondered what the letter could possibly say. All she had to do was talk to Angela, and she would have her answers, but she needed to be sure she could handle it. She wanted the letter; she wanted to know what was left to say after all he'd done.

Being in Johannesburg since end of the trial, Jaines had experienced an awakening of a part of herself she had never known before. She was bold and confident. At the university, she was making friends and building new bonds with strangers. She was openly talking in groups and taking charge of new organizations. For eighteen years of her life, she had been a victim. But she was now beginning to feel victorious. Even though she lost the trial, she found solace in knowing she was truthful. Deep down, she always believed that somehow justice would be served for her. She just didn't imagine justice coming so soon.

"I just wanna dance with somebody," her ringtone blared, the voice of the late Whitney Houston coming through her phone's speaker as she rushed to answer.

"Hola, chica!" burst the sound of Elizaveth's voices in Jaines's ear. Jaines could hear the smile in her tone.

"Sister! What the heck are you doing up, girl?" Jaines asked, wondering how she managed to call her so early in the morning, given the six-hour time difference.

"Chica, I'm finally finished with finals. I miss you. We need to catch up."

"Yeah, we do. I know you've heard the news."

"No. What news?" Elizaveth inquired, having been unaware

of the headlines. Elizveth was away in college, studying hard for her freshman year finals, and had been disconnected from social media. She hadn't talked to Jaines much since the trial ended.

"Otis is dead!" Jaines stated with excitement in her voice.

"Chica, you are lying," Elizaveth stated, in shock.

"No, girl. He really died, but I don't know how yet. We are waiting for the details. Guess what else?"

"OMG. I can't even deal. What else? What else?!" Elizaveth exclaimed, eager to hear what other bombs Jaines had to drop.

"Apparently, he left a letter for me to read. I don't know if I am ready to read it though."

"Sister, what are you going to do? I understand if you don't want to read it." Elizaveth tried to show sympathy, but deep down, she wanted Jaines to read the letter for closure and to see what the creep had the audacity to say. "I mean, if you don't read it, then you will always wonder. Closure is key. Rip the Band-Aid off, sis."

"I know. I need to just read it and get on with my life," Jaines agreed with her best friend since ninth grade, knowing she always had her best interest at heart.

"I will support you in any way! You know I got you, always!" Elizaveth assured Jaines as they wrapped up their girl talk.

The night breeze crept through the open kitchen window as the sun set on the luxury townhome Angela and Jaines shared. It was a warm mid-summer night; Angela felt the joy of dusk as she danced her way around the kitchen from cabinet to cabinet, searching for the right spices and cookware to prepare dinner. The wind lightly caressed her natural curls as she twirled towards the cupboard to grab the turmeric, then towards the counter for fresh garlic cloves. Tonight, she was making her famous curry goat, which was mediocre at best, but she loved the process of making something better each time. Lost in the sound of her own humming, she could not hear the soft sound of Jaines's voice in the distance attempting to break her out of her reverie.

"Angela … Ang!" Jaines called from the doorway of the kitchen to no avail. Jaines moved in closer for better range, only to be swept up in Angela's groove as she grabbed her by the hand and spun her into an uninvited salsa meringue. Angela was fully engulfed by the magic of the evening air, leading Jaines from spin to spin before thrusting her into a back dip.

"Angela!" Jaines screamed in frustration midway down.

"I WANT THE LETTER!" Jaines yelled. She and Angela now stood face to face, hand in hand, toe to toe.

The sound of Jaines's voice interrupted Angela's blissful soiree. Her mood instantly shifted, knowing she would be the one left picking up the pieces of Jaines's broken heart after reading Otis's last words.

"Are you sure you want to do this? You don't have to, Jaines. We can just move on!" Angela said, her voice sternly elevated implying this was not a suggestion but an order.

"No, Angela! I am an adult now, and I can do this. We can do this," Jaines insisted, giving Angela a teary-eyed gaze.

Angela loved Jaines. In her mind, she was the daughter she never had the chance to nurture. She couldn't deny her;, she had seen her through so much and watched her grow. She knew that Jaines was strong enough now. Her fears were not for Jaines but for herself, that she would be the one who couldn't handle Otis's admission of guilt. She had been so focused on Jaines that she ignored her own need to process what she had lost: her husband, her dream life, her daughter, her mother and father. She coped by burying her head in work, taking case after case to keep her mind busy. Now that she was in Africa, every hurt she stuffed away was bursting through the seams of her heart, forcing their way to the surface. One more thing, and she would lose it. Angela had become the master of controlling her environment. But Jaines was a grown woman now, and she had to give her room to blossom.

"Fine. If this is what you want, then so be it!" Angela scoffed before quickly abandoning her second attempt at curry goat and storming out of the kitchen.

Jaines was surprised by Angela's response. She had always been so supportive and was there for every step of this never-ending nightmare. It was hurtful, but it couldn't be a factor in what would happen next.

Startled by the sudden vibrations of his cell phone, he answered.

"Hello? Who's this?"

"Franco, it's … it's Jaines," she said, nerves causing her voice to shake.

"Oh, hi, Jaines," Franco replied. The sound of her voice paralyzed him with the guilt of knowing he owed her so much more than just a hello.

Jaines was still nervous, her palms sweaty as she took a

deep breath, knowing there was no turning back.

"Send me the letter!" she demanded.

TWENTY-TWO

It was 6:00 a.m. in Chicago when Jeston got an unexpected call from Angela informing him of the details of Otis's death. Jeston did not care about Otis and was happy he was dead. In his eyes, death was even too good for him. Jeston had stayed behind in Chicago after the trial and worked on recovering emotionally from the damage left behind by the shitshow he called life. After his attempted murder of Otis, he knew he needed deep work. How could he feel justified in taking someone's life? He was not God; he did not have that power. But in his anger, he did not care, which scared him.

After completing six months of intensive therapy and starting a low dosage regimen of anxiety and depression medications, he was thinking more clearly. He decided to start his studies in business at the University of Chicago and put his intelligence to good use. He'd been hoping to open his own financial advising firm once he finished. The sun was shining again with Jeston; he had made it to the light at the end of the tunnel. Until he heard, "Otis is dead." He knew another round of darkness was on the horizon. The news was already floating around media outlets, with everyone still speculating the cause of death. After finding out that he died by suicide and left Jaines a letter, Jeston had begun preparing his mind for the fallout. The rehashing of the trial and the speculation and scrutiny his sister had to endure might get ugly again. Every time Jaines was in need, big brother came running, and this time would be no different.

"Jeston, since your sister is insisting on reading that letter, I am planning to bring Jaines back to the States so she can do so in the company of close family, friends, and our therapist. She will need us all to be there to support her," Angela suggested to Jeston.

"I think that is a good Idea. There is no limit to Otis's fuckery, and we have no idea what the jackass had to say," Jeston said, fuming at the thought of Jaines having to endure yet another thing induced by their cousin.

"Okay. We will be there soon. Let your mother know," Angela instructed as she ended the call.

———————————

It had been a few days since Jaines requested the letter from the lawyer to no avail. Jaines was fuming with impatience as she and Angela boarded their first-class flight to the States.

"I still don't see why I have to go all the way back to America just to read the letter, Angela," Jaines stated with frustration as she shoved her carry-on into the cabin above their seats.

"Jaines, we've been over this. The U.S. is where your therapeutic team is. We can't expect them to travel here to be there when you open the letter.”

“I am stronger now. I don’t need a support team! I can do this on my own, Angela. You keep treating me like a feeble little child. I am a grown woman,” Jaines sassed as she plopped down in her seat with as much attitude as she could muster.

“Oh, really? A grown woman, are you? Well, a grown woman would understand the significance of protecting her peace at all costs, even if that means traveling a million miles to read a letter left for her by her rapist in the presence of a support team!” Angela yelled with frustration as she shoved her bag under her seat and sat next to Jaines, leaving onlookers stunned by the heated exchange.

Angela immediately felt guilty about her last rebuttal, knowing that Jaines was only scared to face the scrutiny of America. But Angela had been dealing with Jaines’s attitude since the news of her cousin’s death; it was hard trying to make her see things her way. It was a constant battle now that Jaines had a newfound sense of self-worth and power. Angela was happy she was fighting for herself, but she was exhausted being the only one there for her to fight with.

“Listen, Jaines. I know this is scary; this is why we need our community to be with us. I’m only looking out for your best interest. No media will know we are in America. We will quietly land, handle our business, and leave,” Angela said as she tried to settle Jaines’s spirit before takeoff.

“Fine. You win, like you always do!” Jaines scowled as she pulled her eye mask over her eyes and increased the volume of music in her headphones.

Angela rolled her eyes and sighed a deep sigh, in disbelief of how Jaines was handling this. But knowing it would all make sense in the end, she decided not to fight. Leaning her head back against her seat and buckling her safety belt, she closed her eyes and hoped the twenty-hour flight back to America would induce a deep and much-needed slumber.

———————

"Ang and Jainey will be here in less than twenty-four hours," Jeston told his mother as they moved through the supermarket to gather goods for their highly anticipated company.

"We have to make sure we get everything they need so they will not have to leave the house," he urged his mother as they both skimmed the aisles, checking off their grocery list. Jaines requested Hot Cheetos and pickles with sweet red Kool-Aid, a ghetto delicacy she couldn't get back in Johannesburg.

Upon learning of Otis's death, Jeston and his mother, with her insistence, had banded together to be present for Jaines in her time of need. Lainey had been struggling to stay clean while she lived at the sober house. Getting gainful employment, paying bills, and keeping up with her treatment plan was becoming too much for her to bear, not to mention having to actively participate in the lives of her children. They had both given up on her, but she was determined to prove to them that she could be the mother they needed her to be, even though she wasn't so sure of herself.

Lately, her urges had returned, and she had been doing everything in her power to fight them. Though she hadn't yet relapsed, she was afraid one more trigger would push her over the edge. She was still in therapy, learning how to cope with life the sober way, without numbing her pain through drugs and alcohol. It had been almost a year of sobriety, but with the recent news of her cousin's death and the looming final letter, Lainey was feeling the need to escape her reality.

"Finally, we are here! I never wanted to come back to this God-forsaken country so soon," Jaines complained as she and Angela maneuvered throughout the airport to find their Uber.

Since the plane ride scuffle, Angela had decided to be quiet and not respond to Jaines for the time being. She wanted to pick her battles carefully and not use frustration to hurt Jaines. She loved her; she was her baby girl, and her mental health was of the utmost importance. The two of them had survived a lot together, and the guilt of the last thing she said was beating her down.

"Listen, baby girl, I am so sorry about how I spoke on the plane. I didn't mean to use my words as a weapon. I was just frustrated."

"It's fine. I know I've been a bitch lately, but you won't acknowledge my growth, and it pisses me off," Jaines said assertively as she walked a few steps ahead of Angela. Jaines knew she was showing out; she was being bold and standing up to anyone who was getting in her way in life, even though it was Angela, who had supported her every step of the way. She knew she was loved by Angela, but Angela needed to trust her.

She needed to let her make her own choices and stop trying to control every aspect of her life. The thought of her controlling her life enraged her.

"You are just so controlling, and I can't deal with it anymore, Ang. You aren't even my mom. Not even my blood," Jaines said, immediately regretting her impulsivity. The sound of her own words stopped her in her tracks. For the first time in her life, she felt guilty and knew what it was like to hurt someone who didn't deserve it.

She turned to face Angela, who had also stopped mid-stride. Standing face to face, looking each other in the eyes, Angela couldn't fight back her tears. She couldn't hide her hurt. Angela didn't have words to compete with Jaines's newfound sense of courage. She wiped her tears and dropped her head as she recommenced her stride towards their car, lightly bumping Jaines's shoulder as she passed.

Riding in complete silence towards Jeston's penthouse, both women were in deep thought about the task ahead. Angela knew Jaines was exploring her new identity, and she was trying hard to be understanding, not taking her words personally, though they cut like a knife. *This must be what having a teenage daughter is like*, Angela thought to herself as she rode through the sunkissed streets of Chicago.

It was a warm spring day, and the leaves were a vibrant green; the city was bustling with tourists, regulars, and businesspeople. The streets were crowded and congested, traffic moving slowly as the sounds of punk rock lightly played in the background. Usually, she would suggest smooth jazz or old school R&B, but today, she only had the energy to get to her destination. She had been beaten down by this little brat of a so-called grown woman for the last few weeks and was emotionally exhausted. However, she still loved Jaines; she knew she was all Jaines had in this world. Angela was ready to do what needed to be done to close the chapter in their lives once and for all.

The silence between the two was loud, and Jaines could not look at Angela. She felt sorrow for her words and wanted to apologize, but being humble and saying, "I'm sorry," to someone she loved and hurt was a new emotional conquest for her. She didn't quite have the skillset for that. As she sat in silence pondering her recent behavior, she realized maybe she was not as mature as she thought.

"Oh, my goodness! Look at my baby! You are so beautiful!" Lainey screamed as she ran to the back passenger side of the Uber to open the door for Jaines, whom she had not seen since the trial. Lainey hurriedly swung open the car door and reached in, both arms outstretched as she pulled Jaines in for a hug before she could unbuckle her seatbelt.

Jaines had no time to decide if she wanted a hug from her mother.

"Y'all get out. Let me get a good look at you," Lainey said, rushing Angela and Jaines out of the Uber while Jeston grabbed their bags from the trunk. Lainey was in a full-on battle with her urge to get high, but the sight of her baby girl gave her a temporary respite. Jaines and Angela were worn out from the journey and the emotional toil the last couple of weeks had been on them both. But they put on a brave face and smiled, joyfully embracing Jeston and Lainey as they walked into the building.

It had been two days since they arrived in Chicago, and today was finally the day that Jaines would get to read the letter. Back at Jeston's penthouse, the family was waking up to the smell of breakfast being made by Lainey and the sound of smooth R&B playing in the background. Waking up in Chicago was triggering for Jaines, and she had a bad attitude since she'd arrived.

"Jaines, I wanted to talk with you before we head over to the office. Is that okay?" Angela asked as she peeked her head into the guest room.

"Sure, I guess," Jaines said, rolling her eyes.

"Today is a big day. I wanted to see how you are feeling about it all."

"I would be feeling so much better if I could have opened this stupid letter in my own company back in Africa, where I live," Jaines said while looking out of the window, avoiding direct eye contact with Angela.

"I understand, but just remember the past. Look back at our history at how hard it has been. Recall how much we have had to overcome. Now, think of how we overcame it. Did we do it alone? Or did we have help? Community?" Angela urged as she sat next to Jaines, talking to the back of her head.

"Jaines, look at me. You have been disrespectful to me since I told you I had a plan for reading this letter. Initially, I did not want you to read it at all. Otis has put you through enough. But I respected your wishes. Me having a team present is simply having someone on standby to catch you if you fall. I trust you are strong and brave enough, but we don't know what to expect, sweetie, so we need to be prepared for anything.

"You are right," Jaines said, relaxing her shoulders and turning to look at Angela. "It has been hard, and you have been present for me every step of the way. I owe you so much. I just wanted to feel strong and take my power back from Otis. I wanted to prove to myself that I could do this on my own," Jaines said with tears falling from her eyes.

"Baby, nobody is asking you to do that. You have nothing to prove, not even to yourself. Everyone here loves you and wants to support you," Angela said while gently pulling Jaines in for a soft hug. As Jaines laid her head on Angela's chest and smelled her scent, she melted into her embrace; this was the same embrace that had rescued her after her granny died, the same embrace that comforted her many times during the trial. She remembered Angela as her greatest ally, her most loyal friend, her hero.

"I am so sorry for what I said to you at the airport. I didn't mean it," Jaines said as she sobbed into Angela's bosom. Angela quietly rocked Jaines and assured her all was forgiven. After their moment of reconciliation, they enjoyed breakfast with the family before heading to the therapist's office to read the letter.

Upon arriving at the back of the therapist's office, Jaines, Angela, Jeston, and Lainey were all greeted by Otis's lawyer,

Franco. Franco was met with contention as he greeted the group.

"Good afternoon, McGee family. I am so sorry to be meeting you under such circumstances," he said, trying to be cordial despite the awkwardness in the air.

"Whatever, Franco. We don't care for your formalities. Let's just get on with it," Angela snapped.

"As you wish," Franco replied through gritted teeth as he led the family into the building towards their suite.

It had been suspected by the media that the infamous duo had landed back in America since Otis's death, and every gossip influencer was fighting to be the first with an exclusive. Since he died, the trial had been rehashed and played over and over again on major networks. Newscasters all over the world were speculating the cause of death to be something other than suicide, as previously determined by the coroner's office.

"I don't think he killed himself. It had to be that bitter ex-wife who poisoned him, then tried to cover it up."

"Think what you want, but that man had no reason to off himself. He won the trial; he was rich and fine. Why would he need to die? It's a conspiracy."

"I'm willing to bet my entire salary that the little cousin with the funny name had something to do with it. She's just mad she lost the trial."

The media was ferocious with its allegations. Angela and Jeston had been doing their best to keep Jaines shielded from any face-to-face encounters with paparazzi, not letting her leave the house for any reason,and arriving at locations from the back or an inconspicuous place. She was already trying to cope with the erroneous claims being spread about her and Angela. The pair had quietly fled the United States in the aftermath of the trial; the media had been searching for them for months. The only news outlet privy to their location was Stacy Whittaker at Channel 26 News Now, but she had sworn to secrecy because she and Angela were friends.

The family, along with Franco, had finally entered the private therapy suite, where they were greeted by Jaines's therapy team, along with Elizaveth and Andre, whom Angela called in to surprise Jaines with familiar friends. Unfortunately, due to Otis's rule over her life, she had only managed to make two friends in North Carolina.

"Chica, Dios! I can't believe it's you!" Elizaveth screamed with excitement as she and Jaines ran towards one another. Jumping into each other's arms, Elizaveth lifted Jaines to her feet and spun her around while simultaneously jumping up and down screaming, "Yeeeee!"

Upon her release, Jaines immediately ran to Andre and they both wrapped their arms around one another.

"Andre, what are you doing here? I haven't seen you in so long," Jaines said breathlessly with excitement.

"I know. I missed you so much. It's so good to see you!" Andre exclaimed while kissing her on her forehead.

Jaines's family looked on with joy while she became reacquainted with her friends as they each went around the room, shaking the hands of every team member and introducing themselves. After the formalities, the lead therapist began her introduction to set the process in motion.

"Good afternoon to all of you. As you know, we are all here to support Jaines as she faces what may be a difficult task in her life. Our goal here today is to offer a unified front as well as legal advice, but most importantly, a therapeutic approach to whatever Jaines may need during and after the reading of the letter that has been left to her by Otis. Does anyone have any concerns before we begin?"

Jaines felt her stomach muscles tensing as she sat in the middle of the group with Elizaveth at her right hand and Andre at her left, both squeezing her hands in support as the therapist prepped the group.

"I just want to thank you all for being here today," Jaines said with trembles in her voice. As much as she fought against this, now that she was in the room surrounded by loved ones, she couldn't imagine doing this any other way. Jeston was seated next to his mother, who was sweating profusely from nerves and crack cravings. He could see his mother was uncomfortable and offered to escort her out.

"Mama, can you do this? If not, it is okay; we can sit in the hallway," Jeston said, trying to reassure his mother.

"I'm fine, baby. I have to do this for my baby girl. Don't worry about me."

"Good afternoon, everyone. It is an honor to be in your company today, and I will be reading the letter aloud. Does anyone have any objections to my reading of this letter?" Franco stated as he reluctantly looked about the room, scanning for any way out. He never wanted to read the letter, but as Otis's lawyer and the one who aided in Jaines wrongful injustice, he felt indebted to her.

There were no objections …

"Okay. I will begin." Franco, letter in hand, turned to position himself directly in front of Jaines. Looking her in the eyes and clearing his throat, he read:

Dear Jaines …

I cannot imagine the pain that I have caused you. I hate myself for the darkness I have brought upon you in this lifetime. When your mother had you, I was delighted in your presence. You were so cute and adorable. I vowed never to hurt you, and I promised your mother I'd always protect you and keep you safe. Never could I have known that the sickness within me would be expressed in such a way towards you. Please understand you did nothing to deserve my hands on your body. You did nothing to deserve the countless ways I abused you, manipulated you, and destroyed your childhood. I am a sick individual; I have learned that I continued a cycle of abuse that was inflicted upon me as a child in foster care. This is not an excuse to justify my actions, but I hope it aids your understanding as to why this may have happened to you. I pray you get healing, and I hope this letter exonerates you of all blame, slander, and false accusations. I am so, so sorry, and I hope you will someday forgive me. I have chosen to end my life so that yours can finally begin. Everything I have ever acquired in this lifetime, I am leaving to you to use at your disposal. It is nothing compared to what I really owe you, but that is a debt I cannot repay.

With the deepest sorrow and regret,
Otis McGee

The thickness of silence could be felt as everyone in the room was stunned with disbelief. All eyes were on Jaines, who was stuck under the weight of what she'd just heard. Suddenly, she shot up out of her seat, breaking free from the grasps of her friends' hands.

"Franco, you son of a bitch! See, we told you! You knew he was guilty, and you pursued a case against me anyway. Do you know what I went through? Huh?! I hate you!" Jaines screamed as she lunged, hands outstretched towards Franco's neck.

She was immediately intercepted by her big brother, who swept her off her feet and carried her out of the room with the therapist, Angela, and her mother following close behind them.

"Jainey, please take a deep breath," Jeston instructed his little sister, being careful not to tell her to calm down because she had every right to be infuriated. Everyone stood, creating a safe circle around Jaines as she expressed her anger.

"We are all right here, Jaines," the therapist said softly as Jaines slowly dropped to her knees, her face in her hands, and let out the deepest sigh of relief.

"I don't even have any more tears left for this shit. I'm just glad now everyone knows I was telling the truth!" she said through her teeth.

"We never doubted you one bit, baby," her mother said in

reassurance while everyone else agreed in unison.

Angela was shocked by the letter. The admission of her ex-husband in his own words had taken her voice, her strength. She felt weak to her knees but tried to focus on Jaines.

"Jaines, our goal is to make you comfortable. Would you like to stay in the hallway, or do you feel as if you can return to the room? We can also ask the lawyer to leave."

"No, let him stay. He needs to feel this. We can go back in," Jaines said assertively.

"Jaines, let me—" Franco tried to speak. As the group reentered the room.

"No, you've said enough. You knew factually that your client, Otis motherfuckin' McGee, was a monster. You knew what he did to me, and you willingly represented him. Now, you have the fucking audacity to be standing in this room in front of my family on his behalf."

Jeston grabbed Jaines's hand and gently caressed her back in support. He could see her pain. He wanted badly to make it all disappear, but he knew his sister needed her moment to express herself freely. As much as he wanted to interject and knock Franco out, he held it in and let his sister do her thing.

"You tortured me on the stand, Franco, made me look like a liar. Do you know how hard that was for me? To come to court every day and look Otis in the eyes, knowing he was going to get away with molesting me?" Jaines yelled as she stood face to face with Franco, who shamefully had his head down, refusing to look at her.

"Look, Jaines, I deserve all of this. I really do. But please understand I had a job to do. I simply did it. I just represented my client like he paid me to do. None of it was personal; it was just business. I'm so sorry for what all of this has done to you. I hope you can forgive me for my role in this one day," Franco said as he abruptly grabbed his briefcase and ran out of the room.

"Coward!" Jaines yelled to the back of Franco's head as he fled.

Silence fell over the room as Jaines returned to her seat. The lead therapist allowed silence to ensue for a few more minutes before breaking in.

"Jaines, how would you like to proceed? We can end the meeting now and allow a few days before we reconvene to process your emotions, or we can continue while they are still fresh. It's up to you."

"I would like to continue. Because when I leave here today, I will never look back at this," Jaines said firmly.

Before the therapist could proceed, Angela abruptly left the suite to get some fresh air, with Lainey following close behind. Jaines looked on in curiosity but decided not to follow. Her goal was to get through this moment regardless of how hard it was.

"Angela, girl, are you okay?" Lainey asked as they exited the building onto the back steps.

"It's fine. Just a lot to process, ya know? This was my husband. I made love to him. And he was a pedophile. I'm disgusted," Angela said bent over, hands on her knees, waiting for vomit to come up any minute.

"Don't be too hard on yourself. He deceived us all," Lainey said softly while rubbing Angela's arm. "None of us knew how troubled he really was. He hid it very well. There is no way you could have known with all of your travel for work, you know," Lainey continued, unwittingly inciting a fire.

Angela was taken aback by her attempt at consoling her. What was she trying to say? That it was her fault for always being gone for work, that she should have known what was happening? Angela was infuriated at the unintended shade.

"Bitch, I know *you* are not talking. You have never done anything but cause trouble for your own daughter. If it wasn't for you, Otis would have never gotten his hands on her. I've done EVERYTHING for her. She's not even my own flesh and blood, and I love her more than you ever could!" Angela yelled as she stood straight up and turned to stand face to face with Lainey, who was dumbfounded from simply trying to comfort Angela. The insecurity caused by guilt was clouding Angela's judgment. Suddenly, everybody was an enemy.

"Where were you during her trial, huh? Where were you when he was violating her? Somewhere with a fucking needle in your arm!" Angela yelled, enraged, as Lainey stood in shock and at a loss for words.

"Listen, Angela, we all have our part to play in this. The only victim here is MY daughter. Nothing that you have done for her will ever change the fact that she is MINE. You helped her when I couldn't. What do you want, a cookie, bitch? A trophy?!" Lainey struck back at the audacity of Angela to challenge her when she was only trying to help.

Angela, fueled by guilt and shame, slapped Lainey in the face, starting a brawl. Lainey, stunned by the sting of pain across her left cheek, instinctively grabbed Angela by the hair, yanking her head back and forth. But her small, embattled frame was no match for Angela as she punched Lainey in the stomach and shoved her to the ground. The sound of Lainey's body smacking into the pavement knocked Angela out of her rage, and she immediately ran to help her up.

"Oh, my God! Lainey, I am so sorry. I don't know what came over me!" she insisted.

"No! No! Get away from me, you crazy bitch!" Lainey screamed as she got up from the ground and staggered away. "You stay away from me. All of you just leave me alone!" she cried, running from the parking lot.

"Shiiiiiiit!" Angela screamed as she chased after her, knowing this could possibly trigger a relapse. Quickly catching up to her, she grabbed her by the arm and wrapped her in a tight hug. "Lainey, please forgive me. I didn't mean to hurt you."

"Get off of me, Angela, before I call the police!" Lainey yelled as she struggled to get out of her embrace.

"Lainey, please don't leave. Jaines needs you right now. Please. Let's just get through this. You have every right to poison my drink or put sugar in my tank later, but let's just get through this," Angela begged between deep inhales, attempting to catch her breath. "For Jaines. Please!" she pleaded.

Lainey aggressively jerked out of Angela's embrace, heading back to the session and warning Angela this wasn't over. "You better sleep with one eye open, you stupid bitch."

TWENTY-THREE

Walking back into the session, Angela and Lainey tried to pretend as if they were not just fighting, but they couldn't fool the group as Jeston jumped and ran to his mother's aid. Lainey, fueled by adrenaline, hadn't noticed she was bleeding on her elbow and had a tear in her pants from the fall.

"Mama, what the hell happened to you?"

"Oh, nothing, baby. I was trying to console Angela, and I tripped and fell down the stairs. I'm fine. Angela helped me up," Lainey lied as Jeston helped her to her seat.

"Ms. McGee, we have a first aid kit that should clean that right up," the therapist offered as she left to grab it from the supply closet.

Jaines was suspicious of Angela's silence and noticed her hair was disheveled, which absolutely never happened. Besides, it was just fine before she went outside. She knew something was wrong but decided to ignore it for now.

"You know, I really just want to get this over with and go have brunch," Jaines said, trying to break the awkward silence.

"Oh, yeah. They just opened up that new place not far from

here. We should go," Jeston suggested, seemingly oblivious to the obvious tension.

"Okay, let's see that scratch. Looks like the pavement got you pretty good," said the therapist as she kneeled beside Lainey to patch up her wound. "You can fix those pants with a quick little stitch too," she suggested.

"While you all were outside, we discussed the matter of Otis's fortune with Jaines and how she wants to proceed with it. She has decided to take a few days to make her decision while consulting with legal counsel. Mrs. McGee, we are assuming you will provide that counsel?" the therapist inquired while turning to face Angela.

"Um, yes. I will seek an outside source to represent her financial affairs due to the direct conflict of interest," Angela stated, her voice quavering, still frazzled from the scuffle.

"Okay. Well, we are going to wrap up our session here today and allow Jaines some time to individually process her emotions. We plan to reconvene next week before you head back to South Africa."

As we left the session, I could feel a ball welling up in my throat. I knew that I had a big decision to make. This crazed abuser left me his fortune. I could possibly be set for life. Never have to work again. But at what cost? My innocence? My childhood? My pride wouldn't let me accept his money, but my logic wouldn't allow me to willingly let it go either. I had a lot to think about.

"Hello! My name is Anna, and I'll be taking your orders today," a dainty and scantily clad waitress stated as she handed menus to the group, which included Jaines, her brother, her mother, and her two friends. Angela had decided she needed some space to clear her head and took a separate car to "somewhere serene."

"Mama, tell me again how you fell down at the office," Jeston inquired, not initially believing her story.

"Yeah. That whole thing was weird, and Angela's hair was messed up. If I didn't know any better, I'd think y'all were fighting," Jaines insisted.

"Yep. That whole vibe was weird when y'all came back in. I noticed that too," Elizaveth added her two cents.

"That crazy bitch attacked me. That's what happened," Lainey said. "She's losing her mind. All this shit going on with Jaines and Otis is too much for her. She is pretending she's okay, but she's not, and she took that shit out on me today. If it wasn't for all she's done for the two of you, I would have beat her ass," she said with frustration, trying to make them all understand her plight.

Jaines was visibly upset at the thought of Angela attacking her mom, but she was also confused because Angela had never shown one ounce of aggression towards her in her entire lifetime. *She must be suffering in silence; she's too egotistical to ask for help.*

Jaines suddenly felt guilty as a rush of emotions flooded her, remembering all of the sacrifices Angela had made for her over the past few years. She never once thought to stop and ask her if she was okay, if she needed anything. After all, she'd lost her fairytale. Her prince charming was an evil tyrant. She wouldn't get to have his children or grow old with the man of her dreams, the man who was truly a nightmare, a pedophile. And now he was dead. Angela got no closure, no answers, nothing, not even his fortune.

"Oh, my God, I am so selfish. I have to find Angela," Jaines said as she suddenly shot up out of her seat and ran outside to call her cousin.

Angela, who was on her way back to the house to pack her bags, had decided she'd had enough of Chicago and needed to go back to Johannesburg immediately. She was suffocated under the Chicago air — too many bad memories, too many emotions to process. She needed to escape. Before making it home, she remembered she had to pick up a package that had been delivered to her from Franco.

"Pull over here, please. I'll just be a second," she stated as she quickly exited the rideshare to run into the Pack & Ship. In her haste, she had forgotten to grab her shades and wide-brimmed hat, which she wore to remain inconspicuous.

"Hey, lady! Are you … Hey, are you Angela McGee?" she heard as she was walking into the store, which prompted her to pick up her step, lightly jogging inside while covering her face. But the desperate onlooker was in an eager pursuit.

"I dont know what you're talking about," Angela insisted as she continued her light run into the store, quickly making it to the counter.

"Hi. Listen, I have a package. Please scan my QR code. Can you hurry?" she pleaded with the clerk at the counter, with the onlooker now directly behind her, pulling out his phone.

"Hey, y'all! What up, what up! It's ya boy Petty Pete with *All That Gossip*. I am live, y'all. Live in Chicago with Angela McGee! Y'all, look at her. The ex-wife of the late Otis McGee is right here. Y'all been looking for her. Well, here she go!" he yelled into his phone while shoving it into her face and ignoring her personal space.

"Listen, sir. Please get away from me, or I will have to use physical force," Angela warned the infuriating blogger while lightly shoving him back.

"Oh, not physical force, y'all. What you gonna do to me, Mrs. McGee? Kill me like you did your husband?"

Enraged, Angela threw a hard punch directly at the blogger's face, knocking him to the ground and sending his phone flying across the room.

"I warned you!" she said while standing over the blogger, who was flat on his back with his hands covering his face.

"I think you broke my nose!" he screamed as blood rushed down his face, seeping through the crevices of his fingers.

"I told you to move!" Angela yelled back firmly before turning to grab her package, then running out of the store.

"Hurry up. Let's go. Please get me out of here," she stated to the driver, exasperated but slightly exhilarated. Two assaults in one day. She was on a roll. She laughed to herself in disbelief as they sped down the block.

Jaines was growing increasingly frustrated since Angela wasn't answering the phone. She, Elizaveth, and Andre were now standing outside of the restaurant, trying to think of where she could have gone, when Jeston came running out, phone in hand.

"Look at this!" he yelled in excitement, handing Jaines his phone. "She knocked his ass out."

"Oh, my gosh, is that Angela?" Jaines said in shock. "Yo, I

can't believe she knocked dude out like that! Damn, she's knocking everybody out today. We gotta find her before she gets hurt. Let's go," she instructed the group as they gathered their things and headed towards the car.

———————————

"Angela, where are you?" Jaines asked in frustration, finally getting ahold of her.

"Listen, Jaines, I have had enough of all of this. I am going home to Johannesburg, where I belong. Are you coming or not?!" Angela screamed into the phone, clearly having a nervous breakdown.

"Angela, this is not like you. Tell us where you are," Jaines begged, in fear that she would do something irreversible.

"I am fine, Jaines. I am headed to the house to get my shit and get out of this country. ARE YOU COMING?" Angela demanded an answer from Jaines, the tone in her voice hurting Jaines's feelings. She had never experienced an uncontrolled Angela. Fear crept into her mind as she wondered how to handle her. How to respond to her anger. Angela was always her hero, never her antagonist. At this moment, she felt like an enemy.

"Angela, that was not the plan. We came here on a mission. I know this is hard for you, but I need you right now," Jaines said softly, trying to reason with Angela's pain.

Angela immediately hung up the phone.

"Hello? Angela? Hello?" Jaines said. "I think she hung up on me, y'all."

Jaines realized this was bigger than her. She would not be able to reason with Angela now; she had to let her go and focus on being strong for herself. The pendulum was shifting, and her hero was now in need of rescue.

Folding under the weight of Otis's confession, Angela realized she had some unfinished business. "Take me here instead," she instructed the driver, showing him the coordinates to her next location.

Pulling up to her stop, Angela was incensed with anger and sadness. "Please don't leave. This will only take a minute." Angela had already tipped the driver over two hundred dollars, knowing she was going to keep him busy for the afternoon.

Exiting the car, she was met with a warm midday breeze. The sun shined bright in her face, causing her to squint her eyes as she cast her gaze out amongst the graves. She had been given Otis's burial information by Franco over the phone while he informed her of the package he'd sent of her ex-husband's things, along with other unbelievable keepsakes the sick bastard hoarded before he died.

According to Franco, his grave had fresh, only having been buried less than a week ago. She figured she should be able to easily locate it. "It's off to the left of the first curve, near the back of the graveyard, right next to a massive black marble headstone covered in plastic white flowers," she whispered to herself, repeating Franco's instructions out loud.

"Aha! There's the big black headstone, white flowers, and there is the freshly manicured grass," she said as she locked in on Otis's grave and made a beeline in that direction, suddenly sprinting full-speed she abrutptly stopped and thrust herself to the ground at the foot of his grave, her knees plunging into the soil.

"I hate you, Otis. You bastard. Look what you did to us!" she screamed, sobbing and punching the soil. "I gave you the best of me, and what did you leave me, huh? Fucking shame. A legacy of fucking shame," she cried, falling over to her side and balling up into the fetal position, years of pent-up frustration beginning to pour out of her. She grabbed her knees and squeezed herself tightly, crying out loud in anguish.

"You really did that to Jaines, Otis. How could you?" she said in between sobs.

Angela had fought hard in her life to keep going. She pushed through having her own baby ripped from her arms, leaving her parents, and fending for herself her whole life. But this was the last straw. Otis was her knight, a man of valor. She idolized him; she couldn't believe she missed all the signs that he was sick in his head. That he had a lust for kids. She suddenly pushed herself up from the ground, wiping her tears.

"You sick bastard. You think you can just ruin my life and leave?!" she yelled while hiking up her skirt and quickly pulling down her pantyhose. Squatting over the unsettled dirt, she angrily pinched her panties in the middle and, without remorse, slowly unleashed her full bladder on Otis's grave, making sure to release every drop.

"You're not even worthy of my piss. I hope you burn in

hell," Angela scoffed before spitting on his grave and taking a somber walk back to the car. The driver, who couldn't believe what he had just witnessed, somehow respected her and feared her all at the same time.

"Where to now, Miss Lady?"

"Take me home."

TWENTY-FOUR

Pulling up to Jeston's house, Angela was disgusted with herself; she couldn't believe she had lost control of her emotions. She had never allowed herself to become this unhinged. Her entire M.O. was control. She had everything in order around her. But this letter was the end of any ounce of unspoken denial. She'd lost control the moment Jaines tried to commit suicide; since then, her fairy tale had been becoming dismantled piece by piece.

"Angela! Where have you been? We have been calling you all day. You assaulted a man? It's all over the internet!" Jaines screamed at Angela as she exited the car, tears streaming down her face, and sprinting to her. "Are you okay? We were all so scared for you," she expressed while grabbing Angela by her shoulders and shaking her.

"Jaines, I am fine, I promise. I just needed to let off some steam. Now, are you ready to pack your shit and get out of here? I am not staying in this God-forsaken country another day!" Angela asked while shrugging Jaines's hands off of her shoulders.

"Look, I am not doing this with you, Angela. I told you we have a plan, and it's almost finished," Jaines rebutted standing up to Angela

"Yeah, yeah, yeah. 'A plan.' Can't you see this shit is worthless? Huh? We are wasting our time here. We got what we needed; everything else can be done over the phone," Angela said with frustration as she pushed her way past Jaines and headed into the house, carrying the large box of things left by Otis.

"Where are your mother and brother? I need to show all of you what this sick son of a bitch left us," Angela scoffed, not knowing that the scuffle between herself and Lainey today proved to be just the trigger Lainey needed to forsake everything she had overcome in rehab.

"I haven't seen my mom since you assaulted her earlier. Yeah, she told us the truth. What the fuck has gotten into you?" Jaines yelled, following Angela into the house.

Angela was still seething from the admission of her husband. She didn't care that they knew she hit Lainey. All that mattered to her was getting to the contents of this box and getting on the first plane out of America. Sitting down on the couch next to Jeston, she began opening the package titled "For the McGee Family Only."

"Angela, why are you ignoring me? What is happening to you?"

"Jaines, shut up. Please. Just sit down and listen to me," Angela demanded.

Jaines was in disbelief at Angela's tone, but she obeyed, sitting on the adjacent end of the sectional next to her brother with a look of confusion on her face. "Jeston, what's going on?" she asked softly.

"Sis, I have no idea. I guess we are about to find out," he

replied jokingly, trying to lighten the mood.

Angela opened the package and began taking out documents and envelopes. Then came a book that looked familiar to Jaines.

"Wait, is that my diary? He told me he burned that," she said as she reached over and took the diary from Angela's hand.

"Dear Angela, I promise I did not do this because of you. I was only trying to get away from Otis. You don't know who he is. He has been hurting me, and I don't want to be hurt anymore. I love you. From Jaines," Angela read aloud from a piece of paper she had taken from the box.

"What the fuck was that?" Jeston interjected angrily.

"My suicide note. Before I took the pills, I left a note for Angela and Elizaveth. I must have forgotten about them," Jaines said while clutching her diary to her chest.

Dumping the box over onto the floor, Angela revealed more disturbing evidence against the culprit: Jaines's old underwear that Otis had kept as mementos, along with an old cell phone of hers. Each person in the room — Angela, Jaines, Jeston, Andre, and Elizaveth — all sat in silence at the discovery. Since the morning meeting with the therapy team, everything around Jaines seemed to be falling apart, and she still hadn't had time to figure out what to do with her new fortune — or if she wanted to accept it at all.

The group was in disbelief at how disgusting Otis had been to keep reminders of his abuse. After reeling over the contents of the box, Jaines decided she wanted to burn it all. Gathering herself, she stood abruptly to grab the things off of the floor, but Angela put her arm out to stop her.

"Don't touch any of this. Here, give me that diary," she

instructed as she picked the items up one by one and put them back into the box for Jaines.

"I have some lighter fluid, and there is a metal bin in the back. Let's burn all of this shit," Jeston said. He must've been a mind reader because he said exactly what Jaines was thinking. Big brother was always rescuing her. The group swiftly moved to the backyard, where Jeston began preparing the fire. Jaines had been sick to her stomach seeing her old things. This made her relive almost every abusive encounter.

"Jaines, come here, baby girl." Angela instructed. "Do you want to keep any of this?"

"Just my diary."

"Fine. Here, take the rest and dump it," Angela guided her.

"Elizaveth, record this moment. I dont want Jaines to ever forget the day she burned the remnants of her past. Today marks the beginning of something new, something fresh and free. From this day forward, baby girl," Angela said while grabbing Jaines's hand and looking her in the eyes. "It is up to you what happens to your life. You hear me? NOBODY has to ever hurt you or control you again. Now, throw that shit in the garbage where it belongs!"

As Jaines dumped the contents of the box into the bin, Jeston drenched it with lighter fluid. Before striking his match, he turned to his sister. "Jainey, you are a soldier, a bravehearted little girl." With the strike of his match, he tossed it into the bin, igniting a burst of flames that lit up the evening sky.

One week later …

After burning the nightmare box of Jaines's things, Angela decided to stay and finish the job she and Jaines had initially come for. She was finally able to regroup and allow her emotions to take a back seat to the priority of determining how to allocate Jaines's new wealth. Since the initial therapy session, nobody had insight as to what Jaines wanted to do with the fortune left to her. Jaines wanted to make this decision on her own. She had been in silence the previous week while trying this new thing that Elizaveth told her about, fasting.

"Listen, chica, whatever issues you have, just give them to God. Fast and pray, and He will guide you," her best friend had encouraged her before heading back home. Jaines had never fasted before; nobody in her close circle was even remotely close to God, nor did anyone enforce prayer. The deepest spiritual connection she ever experienced was with the spiritual guru when she was a little girl, and her Granny's Sunday morning gospel playlist. But she wanted to try God and see for herself. For the past week, she was only eating once a day and been praying morning, noon, and night for divine wisdom.

"Dear God, forgive me for the distance that I have allowed between the two of us. But I want to close the gap. Please, Lord, help me see what to do. Guide my decisions and my heart during this time. In Jesus's name, Amen."

She prayed the same prayer three times a day for a week. It was now the day of her final session with her legal and therapy team. She was ready to settle this once and for all.

———————————

"What's up? It's ya boy Petty Pete with all that gossip,

ya number one blog for all the shit talkers and celebrity stalkers. It's been almost a week since I was attacked by that vicious bitch Angela McGee. Trust, my legal team is working overtime to get me my coins, honey!"

The punch felt across the world had gone viral, and Petty Pete was determined to cash in on his humiliation. Blogs were even more convinced that Angela was the real reason for Otis's death ; every crime podcast and gossip influencer on social media was adding their own conspiracy theories to the mix. Angela, however, was unphased; she knew the truth.

"Hmmph. I'll be damned if I pay that fool a single dime!" Angela scoffed as she swiped out of the streaming app with one swoop of her thumb and locked the screen on her phone.

She and Jaines were in the back seat of their rideshare, headed to the final meeting. She knew full well that she was prepared to represent herself if she needed to, but it would never come to that. Her firm had already sent a cease-and-desist letter to the blogger, threatening to press harassment charges if he did not leave it alone. After meticulous research, her office confirmed the blogger was broke and could not afford the risk of losing a trial. This would all blow over soon.

"I still can't believe you broke that man's nose. I didn't know you had that in you," Jaines said while chuckling under her breath.

"Listen, I told him to move, and he didn't. So, I moved him," Angela said as they both let out deep belly laughs while slapping their thighs in unison.

The mood between the two had lightened; business was

back at the forefront. Angela's really bad day shed light on the suppressed emotional turmoil she had been enduring. She had agreed to begin talk therapy immediately upon her return to South Africa.

"I am worried about my mother, Angela," Jaines said abruptly, interrupting the giddy atmosphere. "She hasn't been answering my calls since you guys had a scuffle."

"Let me deal with her. I will find her before we leave and sort it all out. She has every right to be upset, but I will make it right. I promise," Angela reassured Jaines as they pulled up and fully stopped at the back of the therapy suites.

Jeston and the therapy team were already there waiting alongside the estate attorney and Jaines's newly hired financial planner, each waiting with anticipation as to how Jaines would allocate her new wealth. Jaines grabbed Angela's hand as the two of them walked down the long corridor towards the door of the suite, the sound of their heels clicking against the floor, echoing off the walls and vibrating in their ears. Jaines was firm and confident in the news she was about to deliver; Angela was prepared to respond accordingly.

"Jaines, Angela, welcome," the lead therapist immediately greeted them upon entry. "We are all delighted to be here with you today. Have a seat wherever you feel comfortable." She continued as she introduced the parties in the room, "Jaines, we are here for you to discuss what you have decided to do with your fortune. Have you been able to make any decisions?"

After taking a deep breath and scanning the room for a spot to focus my eyes — I had heard this is a good way to ease the anxiety of speaking to an audience — I stood, script in hand and nervous sweat pooling underneath my armpits. I took a deep inhale while looking at the ceiling and clearing my throat.

"I first want to thank all of you for being here to support me. In many ways, this journey has been very lonely, but I know that I have never truly lacked the support of those who really matter. Becoming an instant millionaire to any person would be a tremendous shock and a huge blessing. But for me, it is a burden, one that I do not intend to carry. Thankfully, my dear cousin Angela started a trust for me years ago, and I do not need any of the money or businesses left to me by my abuser. With that being said, I have decided to allocate his wealth as follows:

To my brother, I give all of Otis's businesses both local and internationally to do with whatever he pleases, including but not limited to total liquidation, along with all earned revenue generated by said businesses and all owned shares, seats, and positions on company boards. To my brother, I also give all physical property in the form of cars, planes, and all other possessions, as well as all local and international commercial real estate. To my mother, I give every property in the form of a homestead, shelter, or any livable space that he owned for her to do whatever she pleases, along with twenty million dollars to be monitored and managed under a conservatorship, and only to be used if she is clean, sober, and able to pass frequent and random drug tests. If she tests unclean twice within a three-month period, she will relinquish all remaining monies to a rehabilitation facility of her choice. Should she be unable to choose, one will be chosen for her by her managing conservator. For my best friend, Elizaveth,

I will use a portion of his funds to pay her college tuition in full and fully fund all of her educational endeavors for the rest of her life, as well as give her ten million dollars to do with whatever she pleases. To my greatest ally, Angela, I leave the rest of Otis's fortune: those monies in his savings, checking, trusts, certificates of deposits, money markets, and other investment accounts to do with whatever she pleases. For the record, I want it to be known that I do not want a dime of the wealth he accumulated during his lifetime or after, as it is indeed not enough to repay me for what he took from me. Thank you."

Silence fell over the room, but it was soon disturbed. The sudden vibrations of clapping resounded from the hands of my superhero big brother, which was followed by more clapping from everyone else in the room. As they stood and showered me with adoration one by one, each came to hug me or shake my hand as I made my way back to my seat. I could feel the weight of the world lift from my shoulders, knowing that I had defeated the master narcissist at his own game. Not taking Otis's fortune now or ever was a big risk. The money Angela had in my trust was abundant but nothing near what he'd left. But I could not fathom living a life of luxury provided by a man who once forced me to pee in a can.

I was pleased with my decision to hand over the fortune to those who really needed it. I didn't want pity from a monster. His admission was the only vindication I've ever wanted. As far as I was concerned, it was over. All I needed to do now was heal as much as I could and move on with my life. I took a deep inhale, looked about the room, and exhaled. Every anxiety was gone. I was free. The public opinion no longer mattered. I was ready to face the world and become my own person.

____

Lainey had been hiding away in her apartment for the last week, ignoring all attempts at being contacted. Being assaulted by Angela and watching the madness of Otis's confession unfold was all too much. She had her own problems with Otis and her own story to tell, but she had already promised herself she would take it to her grave. However, she needed an escape; her emotions were forcing her to be responsible and face a reality that was a bit too real for her. She had left her only daughter, whom she never loved properly, in the hands of a man she knew to be filthy. It was truly all her fault, like Angela had said.

Sitting on her couch in complete darkness besides a tinge of light seeping through the crack in her curtains, Lainey tapped her needle before holding it up to the faint light, making sure all bubbles were gone. She hoped to ease her worries and relieve the stress of the recent events. She had done this many times before, but this was the longest she'd been clean. *I should just go for a walk or call my mentor*, she thought, but the craving had already won.

"I only need a little hit so I can relax," she said to herself aloud as she eyeballed the syringe with doubt. With one of the tourniquets in her mouth and the other being wrapped around her left bicep, her confidence was growing. Thumping her her inner arm, she waited for her vein to appear. Since she had been in recovery, her arms and veins had become a bit healthier, and she was happy to see one quickly rise.

"Oh, that's a good one," she said to herself, eagerly anticipating the next step. *I'll give my baby girl a call tomorrow*, she thought before experiencing that long-missed euphoria she once lived for.

———————

Two weeks later …

"Hello?"

"Hi. Is this Jeston McGee?"

"Yes. Who's this?"

"This is the county coroner. We have reason to believe that we have a relative of yours who is deceased."

Jeston, arriving at the coroner's office to view his mother's body, asked coldly, "What happened to her?" as the official slides her lifeless body back into the freezer.

"Well, from what I can tell, it appears to be an accidental overdose. Your mother had traces of fentanyl as well as crack cocaine in her system. She also has some track marks on her left arm, and a used needle was located at the scene. Right now, we only have preliminary toxicology reports, but I'm certain this is the cause."

"Damn. She was doing so good. I don't know how I will break this news to my sister," Jeston said, shaking his head in disbelief. "Thank you, sir." He signed the coroner's paperwork before shaking his hand.

"Hello? Jeston? What's going on?" Angela asked, wondering

why he was calling at such an odd hour. She and Jaines had just landed back in Africa a week ago and were still adjusting to all of the recent changes. Jaines was preparing to return to the States to start her life as an independent adult, while Angela would stay behind and continue her work with Leola's Corner.

"Listen, I have some bad news," Jeston stated matter-of-factly. "My mother is dead. They found her yesterday. Drug overdose."

"What? You— Are you serious? I mean, she was doing so well." Angela felt a knot welling in the back of her throat as she stumbled to take a seat on the ottoman near her oversized bay windows, feeling an immediate sense of guilt for her minor assault and the harsh words they shared just a few weeks ago. "I'm so sorry, Jeston. Is there anything I can do?"

"Yes, actually, there is. I need you to keep this from Jaines for now. It's best she doesn't know."

"Wait a minute. I can't keep a secret like this, Jeston; there's no way. Besides, she would never forgive either of us if we did this," Angela explained.

"I know, but she has been through so much lately, and I just can't imagine what this will do to her. She was so hopeful that our mother would stay clean."

"I get it, but we have to tell her. She has a right to know. Besides, it's better to just rip the Band-Aid off."

"I know, I know. That is what you always say. Let's FaceTime in about an hour and drop the news. I need some time to process this before I tell my sister," Jeston instructed Angela before ending the call.

Angela decided to isolate herself in her room for the next hour to avoid any face-to-face contact with Jaines. She was never good at hiding her emotions and knew that Jaines would immediately know something was off with her. Angela could never lie to Jaines; she loved her too much. Over the next hour, Angela read over some policy laws and finalized some case notes for Leola's Corner.

"Jaines, come here for a minute! Your brother is calling," Angela yelled to Jaines from her office.

Jaines skipped into the room, full of joyous energy at the thought of hearing from Jeston. "My big brother is calling! Wonder what he wants," she said in a jovial tone as she plopped down in the office chair next to Angela's desk.

"Hey, sis. How are you?" Jeston started, trying to break the ice.

"Hey, big head. You know me, I'm livin' la vida loca! What are you doing?" Jaines responded playfully.

"Listen, sis. I have something to tell you, and I might as well get it out. I don't know how to put this in any other way but the truth. And this is so hard for me to tell you, but Mom passed away yesterday. Her body was found unresponsive, and they believe it was from a drug overdose," Jeston explained.

My mom is dead. Drug overdose. What? So many thoughts were racing through my mind as my brother's voice replayed over and over in my head. I tried to imagine my mom's last words to me, but the shock of this news was causing my brain to malfunction.

"Is this a joke? Because it's not funny!" I screamed at the phone as I shot up from my seat, eyes fixed on Angela. I was furious with her. I knew this was her fault. She hit my mom and berated her. She drove her to a mental breakdown. She made her relapse.

"This is all your fault, Angela. You hurt her when you hit her. You pushed her over the edge!" All of my emotions were bubbling to the surface, and I could no longer stand still. I ran out of the room in a full sprint down the hallway, out of the front door, and down the streets of our neighborhood.

"Jaines, come back!"

I could hear the sounds of Angela and Jeston screaming, but I didn't care. I just wanted to run as far as I could for as long as I could. Me and my pain; my terrible, sad life. My pathetic existence. No matter how far I ran, I could not escape the reality that being me was a recurring nightmare. One terrible circumstance after the other. My life was a letdown marathon, and I was exhausted. *How much more can my heart take? It's too hard to live.* I wanted to die. I pondered all the ways I could while I was running to the end of nowhere.

"Jaines, stop."

Suddenly, I heard the voice of Angela yelling in my ear, along with the sound of tires screeching next to me. She had jumped in her car and came after me, but I didn't care. I just kept running, ignoring the sound of her door slamming behind her and the thumps of her footsteps swiftly approaching behind me. I had forgotten how much of an athlete she was from all her years of equine therapy.

As much as I thought I was giving running my all, I was no match for Angela, who had quickly caught up to me and suddenly snatched me into her arms. Something about her embrace always made me snap right out of self-pity and remember I am loved, but today, I was prepared to fight that feeling.

"Let me go," I begged as I wiggled and pushed, trying to break her embrace.

"Jaines, I know you are hurting, but please, this is unsafe. Let's just get back home, okay?"

"Leave me alone, Angela!" I screamed as I used all of my might to push out of her grip, finally breaking free and looking into her eyes. "I don't need you anymore" I screamed with every vibration of my vocal cords. Those words broke her. I could see it. Her body tensed up, and her face became distressed. Tears welled up in her eyes.

"Jaines, I know you don't mean that. You are just upset. You have every right to be. Now, let's go home." Angela was growing weary as the threat of danger increased with every inch that the sun set. It was now dusk, and nightfall was on the horizon. We were beginning to draw a small crowd of nosy onlookers.

"Angela, I don't want to go with you. Just leave me alone. I can take care of myself."

I knew full well that I couldn't. I had no resources, and my closest friend from the university lived miles away. I really needed her, as much as I wish I didn't. But I was older and stronger now, and my sense of pride had taken a life of its own. I could not be convinced that Angela was not an enemy.

"You killed my mother! You pushed her to her death!" I yelled, completely overcome with grief.

"I'm sorry, Jaines. This entire thing has been hard on everyone. But we can't do this here." Her eyes were pleading with me as the crowd grew larger and closed in on us. I no longer had an escape route.

"Hey! What is going on here, little girl? Are you okay? Do you know this woman?" asked a curious onlooker as the crowd looked on intently, waiting for my answer.

"Yes, it's fine. She is my mother. We just had a little disagreement, that's all," I explained, trying to calm the masses.

"Well, then, go! Stop disrespecting your mother and get in the car. Go home like she says!" shouted an elder while the crowd mumbled in agreement. Angela quickly grabbed me by the arm and gently shoved me into the car. We sped away in silence as I anxiously contemplated how to get as far away from her as I could.

————————

Today was the day. It had been a little over a month weeks since Otis McGee's funeral, and the media was still speculating his exact cause of death. Conspiracy theories were beginning to take on a life of their own. Crime podcasts and gossip enthusiasts were adamant that Angela and I were the culprits. But today, Franco was going to settle this dispute once and for all.

Since the death of Otis and the reading of the infamous letter, Franco had been overcome with guilt. He hated how the media portrayed us and the role he played in my miscarriage of justice. He had been wracking his brain to think of something he could do to make amends with the family and vindicate me. Last week, he had received a video from Angela of us burning a box of keepsakes that Otis had saved as memorabilia. The video was captioned, "burning the pedo box of horrors." Franco could not believe what he was seeing. He was disgusted by the depths of Otis's depravity, but the video was just what he needed to set his plan in motion.

"Hello, Stacy. It's Franco Beezy, Otis McGee's attorney, and I have an exclusive just for you."

Franco ended the call and stared out over the Chicago skyline, the city humming beneath him, unaware of what was coming. He replayed Angela's video one last time—the flames swallowing evidence that should have never existed. This wasn't about clearing his conscience anymore. It was about setting the record straight.

Across town, the Channel 26 newsroom buzzed as breaking-news energy crackled through the air. Stacy Whittaker scanned the files just delivered to her tablet, her expression sharpening. She'd seen moments like this before—the kind that unraveled carefully constructed lies.

"Ten seconds," the producer warned.

Stacy lifted her gaze to the camera as the red light blinked on.

"Good evening, Chicago. It's Stacy Whittaker with Channel 26 News Now, and I have a bombshell exclusive that you will only get here. Today, we received private details on the case that rocked the nation. Just last year, Chicago's very own Otis McGee found himself at the center of an unbelievable scandal, one in which he was proven not guilty based on a jury of his peers. However, some new evidence shows that a jury of his peers may have gotten it wrong. Take a look at this!"

TWENTY-FIVE

Dear Jaines, you WON!

"Damn right, I did," I whispered to myself as I swiped out of social media and leaned back in my beach chair. The comment sections were passing the vibe check lately since the pendulum shifted, which is a stark contrast to the backlash I faced before. I couldn't believe the mayhem that was going on back in the States since Stacy dropped the bomb that I was an innocent victim!

It had been a few months since the video of my family burning the pedo box was posted to social media, and people were still in a frenzy. As if the video wasn't enough, Stacy had gotten the suicide note from an anonymous source, and with my approval, she read it to the world. It was odd hearing it read from behind a TV screen, and even more odd to hear the world's opinion about it.

Of course, there were still the conspiracy theorists who refused to believe that someone like Otis could ever do this. But the vast majority of the public had turned its fickle fandom towards me. Suddenly, I became a warrior, a soldier, the beauty who survived the beast. I went from sneaky, gold-digging killer to

America's princess. I never cared about the public's view. I carried the truth in my loins; I was still battling with the neurological scars of Otis's hands on my body. I knew the truth would persist, as it always does. I couldn't have imagined I'd be this free though. This freedom is a surprise, even the freedom to say no to the media, who was vehemently requesting my appearance for interviews.

After my mother's service, I was completely devastated that she never got a chance to live a life free of addiction. That addiction was the taker of her purpose. But my brother and I needed to let her go; she needed to be free of this world's plight, a plight she was never built to carry.

After laying her to rest, Jeston and I spent a few days in North Carolina, finalizing the sales of Otis's homes and land and other assets. We also finalized a few business deals. Jeston was happy to be a millionaire, and even happier to sell off all of Otis's business and belongings and create his own ventures with Otis's money. It was the ultimate payback for him; the man who chose to walk away from putting a bullet in Otis's head was now vindicated.

I was at peace with so many things — except Angela. We had lost our place with each other. Since the fight in Africa and her not coming to my mother's service, I had decided to give her some space. She needed time away from me; I had dragged her down. She lost herself in fighting my battle, and I had selfishly held her to a standard that would be impossible for anyone. I had to let her go too, so she could become who she was meant to be without me.

We could not recover after the fight, eventually I packed up and headed back to Chicago. I stayed with my brother until after my mother's service and decided to travel the world. I wanted to see more than the peril I had been subjected to. I wanted to know more languages, eat more foods, and hear more music. I wanted to see all I could see. I wanted to exercise this newfound power: the power to choose, and go, and be whoever I wanted to be.

So, here I am, at my first stop on my quest to discover myself.. I do, however, hope that Angela will be mine again someday. She is the only consistency I've ever had. I still need her.

"Babe, how's your cocktail?"

The sweet sound of Andre's voice broke my gaze into the sun. Since seeing him during my sessions with the therapist, we kept in touch. The spark between us had become undeniable. I was finally healed enough and brave enough to explore the tingle that shocked my belly every time he spoke my name. Bravery had been rewarding for me because this was the sweetest connection I had ever experienced. He was kind and gentle. He was a safe place for my heart to learn and grow.

The air in Aruba was clear; the sun was shining. The sound of the waves crashing against the shore was so soothing, and the grip of Andre's fingers interlocking with mine was grounding. The heat of the sun on my skin felt as if it was healing something deep within me. It felt good here. Everything did. The light was beginning to grow within me, and my mind was beginning to shift towards seeing the world as a safer place to simply exist in.

Finally, things were good. Maybe a promise is not a lie, and there are some dreams that can come true. Perhaps hope is not meaningless after all.

EPILOGUE

"Hi. This is Stacy Whittaker. How can I help you?"

"Um, hello. Yes, this is Celeste," said a shaky voice on the other end of the line.

"Hi. Is there something I can help you with?" Stacy asked, curious about why this unknown stranger had the nerve to call her on a Sunday. Everyone who knew Stacy knew she isolated on Sundays to recharge.

"Um, I don't know. I just got your number from a friend. They said you could help me."

"Okay," Stacy said, reluctantly wondering where this was going. "Help you with what, exactly? Wait, who gave you my number?" Stacy had a strict lock on her number, only allowing close friends and peers to have it as a safety precaution.

"I'm sorry. Maybe I shouldn't have called."

"No, wait, it's fine. Just tell me what you need, sweetie," Stacy replied, trying to ease her fears. She could tell this person was young; she still had the lightness of youth in her voice. She was clearly afraid to proceed, which sparked the feisty reporter's interests even more.

"Well, I was told that you could help me. I, um … I had a, um … Well, when I was sixteen, I met this guy, and, um … I, uh … He, uh …" Celeste fumbled over her words.

Stacy suddenly shot up in her seat at an inkling that she knew where this was going. She quickly paused her Sunday soaps and ran to grab her pen and paper.

"Sweetheart, it's okay, really. Tell me what's going on. Whatever you tell me stays with me," Stacy said softly in an attempt to reassure the young girl.

"Uh, okay. Well, I met this guy when I was, like, sixteen, and he did a lot of things to me."

"Okay, Celeste. Do you know his name? Or is there anything else you can tell me?" Stacy pushed.

"Um, yeah, I can tell you a lot. But for starters, his name was Otis."

ABOUT THE AUTHOR

Felicia Moore, is a budding young writer whose work has been featured in several podcasts, magazines, and local libraries. Felicia made her professional debut in 2019 with the release of her exciting and educational children's series entitled "The Adventures of DJ The Boy Genius Vol 1: Hurricane Harvey Ruins The Party." Which has since been featured on Houston's well known news station KHOU-11's Bed Time Stories; and read by Houston's chief meteorologist. Felicia considers herself the type of writer who writes outside of the box, and does not limit herself to any particular genre. She is also a beloved poet and spoken word artist; you can visit Felicia online at www.feliciathepoet.com.

Felicia lives with her son in Houston, Texas.